Delia's Doctors

Delia's Doctors

OR, A GLANCE BEHIND THE SCENES

Hannah Gardner Creamer

Introduction by Nina Baym

UNIVERSITY OF ILLINOIS PRESS

URBANA AND CHICAGO

⊗ This book is printed on acid-free paper.

Library of Congress Cataloging-in-Publication Data
Creamer, Hannah Gardner.
Delia's doctors; or, A glance behind the scenes /
Hannah Gardner Creamer ; introduction by Nina Baym.
        p.   cm.
Includes bibliographical references (p.   ).
ISBN 0-252-02807-4 (cloth : alk. paper)
ISBN 0-252-07108-5 (pbk. : alk. paper)
1. Young women—Fiction. 2. Self-actualization
(Psychology)—Fiction. 3. Depression in women—Fiction.
4. Physicians—Fiction. 5. Medicine—Fiction.
6. Massachusetts—Fiction. I. Title.
        PS1469.C536D45   2003
     813'.3—dc21   2002069552

Contents

knowledge. But, before this can happen in the narrative, Creamer uses Delia to test the day's popular medical therapies, showing their inapplicability to her situation and exposing their more general inadequacies as well.

The most important therapies are standard (allopathic) treatment, homeopathy (treatment through minuscule doses of the supposed disease-causing agent), phrenology (character analysis and recommendations based on skull shape), hydropathy (cold-water treatments), mesmerism (hypnotic cure by suggestion and laying on of hands), Thomsonianism (therapy via steam and other heat-causing agents including pepper and herbs), and a gamut of dietary regimens prohibiting spicy, fatty, stimulating, or intoxicating food and drink. After sampling these diverse options to no avail, Delia is more disheartened than ever. Thoroughly depressed, she anticipates an inevitable decline into early death.

But *Delia's Doctors* is a didactic comedy; a sentimental death scene is not in Delia's destiny. Now, Adelaide Wilmot, the fiancée of Delia's older brother Charles, steps in to deliver the health lectures that the book is designed to validate. As one useless or fraudulent therapy has followed another in earlier chapters, Adelaide has been on hand to analyze each, sorting out strengths and weaknesses, distinguishing false from useful claims, assessing the qualifications and pretensions of the self-styled experts,

and invoking the laws of health that Delia must follow on the road to recovery.

There is little danger that an active temperament
like Adelaide's—or like that of Delia's fourteen-
year-old proto-feminist sister, Ella, who romps
through the novel insisting on the right of women to
do anything they want—will lapse into Delia's melancholy passivity. But although women like Adelaide and Ella may signify what most American
women will become in the future, in a present time
defined by egregious limitations on women's life
options, they are exceptions. While Creamer thinks
their unconventional aims and energies should be
better appreciated, she does not think these women
can serve as models for more ordinary women.

Ordinary women like Delia are faced with the
odd irony that a woman's life in the rising and
expanding middle class, even though it offers un-
precedented leisure and comfort, also denies pur-
poseful, interesting activity. Women have lost the
active roles that occupied their foremothers in a
rural, agrarian culture. The strengthening physical
labor demanded of early farm women is no longer
necessary; gone with that labor is bodily health
along with the satisfying sense of contributing to
family and national life. Delia's mother, for example, is a sour-tempered termagant who enforces
outdated social restrictions on her daughters (she
caters to Delia's every sickly whim and tries constantly to rein in the ebullient Ella) without realiz-

ing how much her own seething discontent is the outcome of these very restrictions.

Just as inactivity leads to ever more debilitation, so lack of belief in one's agency leads to ever more passivity. For Delia and the thousands she stands for, even the seemingly simple act of taking charge and thereby rejecting the tempting but destructive cultural role of female invalid may be extremely difficult. Liberated from menial toil, Delia lies on the sofa all day getting sick from eating too much pastry. She accepts her invalidism and is even somewhat attracted to the invalid's place at the family center. In a culture where women get so little attention, and where what attention they get is so often hostile, playing sick to a doting audience has obvious appeal. The role carries special conviction if the player is really sick. To take charge of one's life requires freeing the inner self from its demands for approval and its masochistic willingness to suffer for love.

So, if *Delia's Doctors* is chiefly about medical matters, it connects this theme to existential dilemmas commonly faced by young white middle-class women. It insists that such women must understand themselves as free and independent individuals capable of making decisions and acting in their own interests. It makes women's freedom and independence inseparable from their health. And, just as healthy women require a society that respects them and gives them many life options, so respected women with many life options will produce a healthy society. Working for one's own health and for the health of one's family and for other women becomes a way of contributing to national progress, a way of acquiring purpose. There is a reason for Creamer's identification of Delia with thousands of "American" girls; it allows her to write a book implicitly about national betterment through an explicit story about private individual self-improvement.

That health is a woman's issue had been recognized at once by the first generation of American feminists. It is no accident that Adelaide, the "doctor" who finally prescribes what Delia needs, is a woman. In the real world outside the narrative many early women's righters (the first women's rights conference took place at Seneca Falls, New York, in 1848) made a specialty of giving popular health lectures to women (a leading example is Paulina Wright Davis, one of the women's rights movement's most active members). Conversely, many among the first generation of women doctors found themselves drawn to feminist activities (a leading example is Harriot Hunt, one of the first women to practice medicine in Boston). As any feminist reader will know, the connection between feminism and women's health continues in force.

Although she eventually published four books, Creamer was not a professional author in the sense of one who made a lifelong career of authorship and enjoyed wide publicity. But *Delia's Doctors*, written with considerable verve and humor in a comfortable prose style, shows her to be practiced and talented at her craft. In the book Creamer adeptly types, with quick, firm, accomplished strokes, each member of the large Thornton family, including the parents and six children ranging from twenty-four-year-old schoolteacher Charles down to baby Georgie. The procession of therapists, the minister, and a few other auxiliary characters are also efficiently outlined. None of these depictions aims at psychological depth; rather, each represents one facet of New England small-town cultural, intellectual, and family life, contributing to a cumulative social portrait.

The literary and theological chatter permeating the book adds to and connects with the themes of medicine and women and thereby conveys a good sense of the materials that would have formed the conversational staples of educated New Englanders at that time. References to poets, essayists, and novelists of the past and present abound. Theology enters as a matter of course; the omnipresence of doctrine in New England intellectual life was a cultural given.

Nor were women barred from doctrinal conversation; from the earliest period they had comprised the majority of church members. Beginning with Anne Hutchinson in the seventeenth century at least some had insisted on their right to promulgate their own religious views. In the increasingly print-centered mid-nineteenth century, women— still mostly denied access to the pulpit (but the year after *Delia's Doctors* appeared, Antoinette Brown. an Oberlin graduate, became a Congregationalist minister and the first American woman to be ordained by a recognized denomination)—published in ever-greater numbers on religious questions. Missionary work around the world engrossed them. Religious and secular concerns formed an inextricable web of discourse; polite literature in particular allowed people to talk doctrine without usurping the minister's role.

Then, too, religious beliefs could not be separated from convictions about women's social place and even about health. How, for example, was the Pauline pronouncement on women's silence in the churches to be reconciled with female religious discourse of any kind? As for health: if sickness registers the outcome of God's inscrutable will or constitutes God's punishment for sin, then attempts to cure an illness become attempts to circumvent divine dispensation—virtual blasphemy. When anesthesia entered medical practice in the late 1840s, many conservative dogmatists opposed it because the Bible ordained that women would bear children in pain and suffering. Thus, women talking about the rules of health challenged the doctor and the minister simultaneously, while women talking about anything other than fashion or gossip challenged every attempt to circumscribe their intellects by keeping their minds focused on vacuous trivia.

———

As a publishing author aspiring only to local fame—if even that—Creamer has left little trace in the literary record. But when one meshes the sparse available facts (including records in the Salem City Hall) with apparent autobiographical asides in her prefaces, conclusions, and narrator comments, one can dimly discern the shape of a recognizable type of New England woman's life. She was born in Salem in 1796, the fourth and last child of Samuel Gardner and Hannah Stevens Gardner. Her parents had married in 1788, when Samuel was twenty-five years old. (At present, her mother's birth date is not known.) Samuel, like so many Salem men, went to sea, became a captain at a young age, and went down with his ship. When he drowned in 1796, he would have been thirty-three years old. The oldest of the four children he left behind was seven; Hannah may not even have been born yet. Here is a familiar, lugubrious New England pattern. The best-known literary example is probably Nathaniel Hawthorne, who was four years old when his sea-captain father died of a fever in Suriname, leaving his widow with three children.

Hawthorne's mother went back to live with her natal family, the Mannings, who reared the whole brood. What Hannah Creamer's mother did as a widow is not known but, in view of the particularly passionate polemics against seamstressing in Creamer's work, she may well have tried to earn a livelihood by sewing at home. This unhealthy work was the chief means of support available to genteel women who lacked formal education. Why is sewing unhealthy? Because—especially in the era before sewing machines—the poor light in which it was carried out damaged the eyes; the physical immobility it required damaged the body; its monotony produced mental vacancy; and the pay was so low that women wore themselves out with ceaseless stitching. Fictional depictions of the struggling seamstress may seem mawkishly sentimental now, but they reflected a grim reality. Sarah J. Hale, for example—as editor of *Godey's Lady's Book* she became one of the nation's most influential women— struggled for several years to support herself and five young children by needlework after her husband succumbed to cholera. She was rescued through the subvention of her initial literary efforts by her husbands' lodge mates. As writer and editor she made enough money to send her boys through Harvard and give her girls the best available education possible.

Whatever her mother may have done, Hannah Creamer did not become a seamstress but took advantage of a newer, more interesting career established for women in the early nineteenth century—teaching. One can deduce from authorial interpolations that she was likely the preceptress of a private academy—a secondary school—for girls. In such a position, she could have boarded students in her home or accepted them as day scholars, living by what she could charge for tuition and board. The record shows her marrying George Creamer in 1822, when she was twenty-six. George died in 1870, Hannah in 1883 at the age of eighty-seven. She is reported to have had children, although nothing about them appears in her author asides. For that matter, nothing about her husband appears either. In her writing she assumes the familiar literary persona of the teacher who lives for her students and functions as a maternal surrogate. In women's fiction, public school teachers tend to be unmarried girls and academy preceptresses tend to be widows, but this does not seem to have been Hannah Creamer's life situation. Possibly her husband, like the spouses of the educators Emma Willard and Willard's sister Almira Hart Phelps, worked with her as financial director of the school and general factotum.

The teacherly persona, in any case, is much in evidence in four of her known books. The first, *Gift for Young Students,* was published in Salem in 1848. George Creamer, who took out the copyright, is named publisher; that the book was set and printed in Cambridge (by Harvard University Press) suggests a self-publishing venture, a book produced for local consumption by friends, acquaintances, and former students. The copy I worked with, from Harvard's library, is a presentation copy signed by the author and inscribed by the recipient to her niece. This is a perfect example of the handing-on of the book that Creamer probably anticipated. In view of the author's age in 1848 (she would have been fifty-two), publication of *Gift* likely signaled her retirement from active teaching.

In all likelihood Creamer had already published short pieces in local journals and newspapers; perhaps the contents of *Gift* had previously appeared in print. *Gift* contains sprightly sketches of varying lengths, wherein women teachers explicate diverse branches of learning and expatiate on the general importance of learning to young people. There are numerous illustrative brief sketches of female students, each developed as an old-fashioned "humor" character (a character defined by one marked trait) to point out a different didactic message. Among the portrait gallery one finds such staples as the overly bookish, the excitably nervous, the phlegmatically good-hearted, the energetically idealistic, the placidly conventional, and the cannily opportunistic. The whole blends vigorous advocacy of learning as character formation with illustrations of the characters a teacher is likely to encounter in her classroom. For Creamer the art of teaching requires configuring the subject to the student's abilities and temperament. This means that teachers must study their students as much as they do their subjects; it means that students *are* the teacher's subjects.

Two books followed quickly after *Gift—Eleanor; or, Life without Love* in 1850 and *Delia's Doctors; or, A Glance behind the Scenes* in 1852. Not for another thirty-five years, and then only posthumously, would another book by Creamer appear. Presumably the 1885 novel *The Household Myth* was brought out by her survivors as an act of filial respect. Thus, Creamer's main literary output is centered around 1850, just when the blockbuster best-selling women's novel became a literary staple and transformed ideas of female authorship.

As far back as the 1790s, and certainly by the 1830s, authorship of some sort had become a woman's opportunity. Certainly writing was better than sewing—Anne Bradstreet had made that point in 1650. For many it also seemed preferable to the demands of teaching a constant stream of unruly and intellectually recalcitrant young people. Research since the 1970s has thoroughly exploded the idea that antebellum U.S. women either did not publish or did so secretly, anonymously, or under the protection of a pen name. The idea of the silenced literary woman was an attractive, perhaps necessary, spur to feminist literary scholarship in the 1970s and 1980s; but this very scholarship has uncovered so much published work by women that we must acknowledge the general acceptability of authorship as a female career.

Women writers and their supporters (editors, publishers, educators) argued that authorship would both develop women's intellect and demonstrate the equality of the female with the male mind. They also argued that, since writing could be carried out in the privacy of the home, women authors would not transgress on male public space. Publishing initiatives by and for women succeeded so thoroughly that Margaret Fuller, writing in 1843 in "The Great Lawsuit" on behalf of women's rights, could point to the press as a domain already securely occupied by women. (Creamer also alludes to women's easy access to print in *Delia's Doctors*.)

But in 1850, a novelistic subgenre specific to women—combining an interesting story centered on the life of a young girl as she approaches womanhood with a series of moral lessons about selfhood—received a powerful impetus in a very long and immensely popular novel called *The Wide, Wide World*. This novel, by Susan Warner, chronicled the struggles of a young girl from a well-off family who is sent to live with an uncouth country aunt because of her mother's ill health. *The Wide, Wide World* merged the moralistic didacticism of women's schoolroom sketches like those in Creamer's *Gift* with the plot-and-character interest of emergent Victorian psychological realism. Warner's protagonist, enraged by the social indignities she suffers and heartbroken over separation from her beloved mother, learns over time to control herself. She discovers that self-control is a means of controlling her surroundings and disarming the hostility of others.

The Wide, Wide World broke all previous sales records for American fiction. Its deceptively simple story, whose everyday heroine did everyday things in local settings among (for the most part) everyday people, inspired numerous imitations. Some of them, like Maria Susanna Cummins's *The Lamplighter* (1854) and, eventually, Louisa May Alcott's incomparable *Little Women* (1869), surpassed the original in popularity. Good domestic novelists invented plots whose ongoing trials and suspended triumphs encouraged young women to identify themselves with the protagonist and therefore to keep turning the pages to see how their own lives would turn out. These novels housed believable, sympathetic characters whose inner struggles communicated a powerful sense that having a rich inner life, for better or worse, was what being human was all about. This meant that those condemned to limited experience by cultural constraints on female mobility were nevertheless profoundly human, a point that Emily Dickinson's poetry began magnificently to enunciate just a decade after Warner's great success.

Schoolteachers who assayed the genre of fiction because of its didactic potential—and many did— were sometimes ill-equipped for novel writing be-

cause their real interests lay in what the books had
to teach rather than in character, setting, or story.
Most of the hundreds of homiletic domestic fictions
published in the twenty years after *The Wide, Wide
World* sank without notice, lost even in their own
time. Hannah Creamer's second book, *Eleanor; or,
Life without Love* (1850), is one of these; yet its
variations on Warner's formula are not without interest. Its protagonist is not sent away from home;
rather, she is loved by neither her monstrously ty-
rannical father nor her passive, intimidated mother.
This parental configuration allows Creamer to
mount a smashing attack on the traditional family
structure. Eleanor, a plain girl with a scholarly bent,
turns to reading for solace. She grows up unloved
and unlovable until various surprising events under-
mine the plot's initial logic, transforming her into a
southern heiress who does good for all (including,
notably, the slaves whom she inherits and manu-
mits). The book ends with an appreciative hus-
band-to-be in the wings. It seems to be aimed at a
special category of young women—those who arm
themselves with erudition less because they care
for learning than because they are lonely and neglected.

Although announcing itself as a novel, *Eleanor*'s
real investment is in idea-laden dialogue, including
many striking paragraphs of abolitionist polemic.
The 1885 *Household Myth* is more novelistically
ambitious, dividing its plot between a New England

household with three daughters (on whose doorstep a foundling is deposited) and southern California, where the contrite father of this foundling succeeds in life by growing citrus for the burgeoning population of Los Angeles. The three-daughter household allows Creamer to develop her multi-temperament view of female human nature. The plot shocker is that the middle daughter, the most conventional and domestic of the three, is actually the mother of the foundling and secretly married to the runaway father. While the logic of the plot is not clear, the logic of making the most ordinary of the daughters the most vulnerable to her emotions is consistent with Creamer's idea that it is the weaker sisters who need the stronger discipline. The California setting and other topical references indicate that Creamer worked on the book after 1870; but though *The Household Myth* continues her theme of women's need for and right to professional advancement, its awareness of women's options seems quite dated. The scholarly protagonist, for example, laments that she cannot have an advanced education; but by the time of Creamer's death, land grant colleges in the Midwest and women's colleges in the Northeast had opened higher education to women. Thus, while all of Creamer's output has something of interest for specialist readers, the focus on health in *Delia's Doctors* makes it a signal contribution to the saga of antebellum female authorship in the United States.

The parade of Delia's doctors begins with a visit from the town's resident physician—Dr. Perry, the allopath, or regular practitioner. This person at midcentury was by no means always a medical-school graduate because there were very few medical schools as such. The college-level medical curriculum, so far as one existed, included physiology, anatomy, materia medica (the therapeutic attributes of plants), and—sometimes—chemistry. Few practicing physicians had taken such courses, since only a tiny proportion of that population had attended college; most doctors had apprenticed informally. Clinical opportunities were unavailable in the United States; one had to go to the great hospitals in London, Paris, Vienna, or Zurich for exposure to the range of pathologies. Doctors needed no licenses, schools needed no accreditation, uniform curricular standards were nonexistent.

The 1840s, a key decade for knowledge production and circulation, saw the formation of the American Medical Association by men striving to protect their reputations from accusations of quackery. But professionalizing strategies such as controlling access to knowledge, increasing the amount of knowledge necessary to become a doctor, accrediting schools, and licensing doctors were quite new when *Delia's Doctors* appeared. Anybody could still hang up a shingle and start a medical practice.

Allopaths, therefore, were known by their therapies rather than their credentials. With the microbial theory of disease not yet articulated (this happened in the late 1860s and early 1870s following discoveries by Louis Pasteur and Robert Koch), allopaths still worked from the Galenic principle that disease resulted from the overproduction of one or another specific bodily fluid. Their therapies strove to restore balance by ridding the body of the offending fluid by bloodletting, purgatives, or emetics. Wise practitioners reserved such "heroic" treatments for serious cases but, sensitive to the patient's desire to be cared for, they often cannily recommended mysterious medications that were really placebos.

Delia's Doctors is not hostile to allopaths, whom it finds well-equipped for treating "real" diseases and setting broken bones. "Oh, these doctors! Give them a patient actually ill in bed, racked with pain, tossed with fever, or raving with delirium, and they are enraptured"; but if they are "summoned to prescribe for a nervous young lady, with no particular disease, who has, or fancies that she has, a thousand contradictory symptoms," they are hard put to suppress signs of contempt (p. 22). What Dr. Perry lacks in psychological finesse he makes up for in unwelcome honesty, telling Delia bluntly that her "palpitations are the result of indigestion, caused by want of exercise, or the use of improper articles of diet" (pp. 22–23). If Delia ate less and walked more, she would get better.

This is not what she wants to hear, however, so

the book then moves on to popular alternative therapies, all of which are less invasive than heroic allopathic remedies and most of which advance one single solution for all illnesses while rejecting the single solutions of other alternative therapies. Their shortcomings might suggest the wisdom of returning to the family doctor—and indeed, at the novel's close all the other self-styled medicine men have left town—but Creamer means for Delia to become her own doctor, to cure herself by learning the laws of health and adjusting her behavior to these laws.

The iterated phrase *laws of life* refers to a theory taking for granted that the natural state of the body in a world created by a benevolent God is health, so that if certain rational (scientific) principles were understood and applied, health and longevity would inevitably ensue. The phrase *laws of life* implies the Enlightenment ideas that the universe is lawful, that people are designed with the capacity for understanding the laws, and that although people are allowed to break these laws, the laws are in fact easily followed. A broken law exacts a punishment that is not meted out maliciously, but educationally, to teach offenders that they have done something wrong. When the laws of health are broken, the punishment is disease. Thus, for all her unconventional self-assertiveness, the active Adelaide is really a law-abiding character and the sickly Delia is the lawbreaker.

That *Delia's Doctors* was published by the New

York firm of Fowlers and Wells fits its laws-of-life orientation. This company specialized in alternative health publications for the general public. The Fowler family endorsed and profited by transmitting knowledge to a population still mainly denied access to formal education beyond the primary level. Fowlers and Wells's best-selling books, by the Scottish phrenologists and physiologists George Combe and Alexander Combe, were laws-of-life expositions. (Adelaide identifies the Combes as sources.)

Those at Fowlers and Wells were especially keen on phrenology. This approach to human psychology enjoyed a brief run in the United States as a serious science before being empirically discredited by the obvious lack of correspondence between external skull shape and internal brain shape, not to mention between external skull and personality attributes. By 1850 it was practiced mainly as a kind of fortune telling or a parlor game and viewed by educated people as a pseudo-science. But today, many historians of science interpret it as an early attempt to bridge the mind-brain gap by placing the ineffable mind quite specifically in the physical brain.

Phrenologists held that no matter how essentially spiritual humans may ultimately be, we function on this earth via material organs. The phrenological mantra was that the brain is the organ of the mind. The way to learn about the mind was therefore to learn about the brain. *Delia's Doctors* says little about phrenology, but what it says is favorable and—more important—clearly adheres to the no-tion that on this material earth we are required to live as material bodies. Its physiological explanation for Delia's depression and anomie asserts that her brain-located mind has been affected by material circumstances. Hers is no spiritual disease.

Given Creamer's strong bias in favor of female activity, it is perhaps surprising that she did not take a stand on women physicians. Around 1850 a strong impetus for training women as doctors had emerged. Before the 1840s no medical school accepted women students; the few that did shortly thereafter tended to be those specializing in alternative therapies. Elite men's colleges remained closed to women, but around midcentury initiatives to prepare women as doctors emerged simultaneously in many quarters. Sarah Hale editorialized in the *Lady's Book* that female delicacy required women doctors; she called the male obstetrician an obscenity. Medical schools for women sprang up in Philadelphia, New York, and Boston. By 1870, women doctors were part of the cultural scene. According to Mary Roth Walsh's study of census figures, some two hundred "legitimate" women doctors (i.e., doctors who were not abortionists) were in practice around 1860, twenty-four hundred around 1880, and more than seven thousand at the century's end. By 1914, for reasons not yet understood, the number had dropped strikingly by over half.

But for fifty years medicine seemed available as a career for women who were prepared to study hard at difficult scientific subjects and work long hours.

This is just why female medical professionalism is of no relevance to Creamer's initiative in *Delia's Doctors*. Certainly, the book has no objection to women doctors; it wants all the professions open to women. But if a woman had to become a doctor to take care of her health, the book's whole purpose would be invalidated.

There is a kind of democratic ideology that believes in the extraordinary gifts of every individual and looks toward a perfect world in which all individuals will become the remarkable persons they are meant to be. Another kind of democratic belief accepts something like "mediocrity" as the normal human state but maintains that even middling people deserve life, liberty, and the pursuit of happiness. Add to this list the recognition that without health none of the others are possible, and one has the approach of *Delia's Doctors*, which also implies that no nobler goal exists for talented women like Ella and Adelaide than helping their more vulnerable and less able sisters, the Delias of the world.

Bibliography

Bayın, Nina. *American Women of Letters and the Nineteenth-Century Sciences*. New Brunswick, N.J.: Rutgers University Press, 2002.

———. *Woman's Fiction: A Guide to Novels by and about Women in America*. 2d ed. Urbana: University of Illinois Press, 1993.

Cayleff, Susan E. *"Wash and Be Healed": The Water-*

Cure Movement and Women's Health. Philadelphia: Temple University Press, 1987.

Creamer, Hannah Gardner. *Delia's Doctors; or, A Glance behind the Scenes*. New York: Fowlers and Wells, 1852.

———. *Eleanor; or, Life without Love*. Boston: James French, 1850.

———. *Gift for Young Students*. Salem, Mass.: George Creamer, 1848.

———. *The Household Myth*. Boston: Charles H. Whiting, 1885.

Davies, John D. *Phrenology, Fad, and Science: A Nineteenth-Century American Crusade*. New Haven, Conn.: Yale University Press, 1955.

Donegan, Jane B. *"Hydropathic Highway to Health": Women and Water-Cure in Antebellum America*. Westport, Conn.: Greenwood Press, 1986.

Fuller, Robert C. *Alternative Medicine and the Cure of Souls*. Philadelphia: University of Pennsylvania Press, 1989.

———. *Mesmerism and the American Cure of Souls*. Philadelphia: University of Pennsylvania Press, 1982.

Gevitz, Norman, ed. *Other Healers: Unorthodox Medicine in America*. Baltimore: Johns Hopkins University Press, 1988.

Herndl, Diane Price. *Invalid Women: Figuring Feminine Illness in American Fiction and Culture, 1840–1940*. Chapel Hill: University of North Carolina Press, 1993.

Kaufman, Martin. *Homeopathy in America: The Rise and Fall of a Medical Heresy*. Baltimore: Johns Hopkins University Press, 1971.

Kett, Joseph F. *The Formation of the American Medical Profession: The Role of Institutions, 1780–1860*. New

Haven, Conn.: Yale University Press. 1968.

Morantz-Sanchez, Regina. *Sympathy and Science: Women Physicians in American Medicine.* New York: Oxford University Press, 1977.

Rothstein, William G. *American Physicians in the Nineteenth Century: From Sects to Science.* Baltimore: Johns Hopkins University Press, 1972.

Starr. Paul. *The Social Transformation of American Medicine.* New York: Basic Books. 1982.

Sterne, Madeleine B. *Heads and Headlines: The Phrenological Fowlers.* Norman: University of Oklahoma Press. 1971.

Verbrugge, Martha H. *Able-Bodied Womanhood: Personal Health and Social Change in Nineteenth-Century Boston.* New York: Oxford University Press, 1988.

Walsh, Mary Roth. *Doctors Wanted, No Women Need Apply: Sexual Barriers in the Medical Profession.* New Haven, Conn.: Yale University Press. 1977.

Whorton, James C. *Crusaders for Fitness: The History of American Health Reformers.* Princeton: Princeton University Press, 1982.

Delia's Doctors

DELIA'S DOCTORS;

OR,

A Glance Behind the Scenes.

BY

HANNAH GARDNER CREAMER.

"It hath a plan,
But no plot. Life has none."—FESTUS.

NEW YORK:
FOWLERS AND WELLS, PUBLISHERS,
CLINTON HALL, 131 NASSAU STREET.

Boston, 142 Washington-st.]   1852.   [London, No. 142 Strand.

DELIA'S DOCTORS.

I.

THE YOUNG INVALID.

"They tell me spring is coming,
  That buds begin to swell;
They bid me trust the warm, bright days
  Will cheer and make me well."—MRS. S. J. HALE.

NEW ENGLAND had been favored with "a moderate winter." There had been, indeed, no want of bracing air and violent storms; but so many mild, pleasant days had been granted, that the sages, who discussed the weather upon 'Change; the editors, who duly recorded its fluctuations in the public journals; and the venerable dames, who regularly compared the predictions of the almanac with the actual state of the atmosphere—all concurred in the opinion, that for many years we had not experienced so warm a winter. Aunt Deborah, a firm believer in the doctrine of Compensation, solemnly shook her head, declaring, with oracular look and tone, "that it made no kind of difference; the spring would be severe enough; and that, take the year through, we must have the same amount of cold, and the same number of storms." Her theory was, this time, verified. The school-boys, who had sighed over the deficiency of snow-balls, rejoiced, as every few days in March and April clothed the earth with bridal array. More than once the streets seemed paved with ice, and the buildings roofed and boarded by the same material. The river was one solid, glacial block. We might have constructed an ice palace, equal in beauty and magnificence to that of the Empress Anna. New England ice would have served as well as Russian. The banks of the North River were as eligible as those of the Neva.

The cold, also, of this memorable spring was so intense and so prolonged, that more than one fair maiden queried whether she were doomed to wear muff and tippet, cloak and India rubbers, till midsummer.

None, probably, longed for warm weather more than Delia Thornton and her alarmed friends. She was not yet nineteen, but her countenance betokened so great a degree of sadness, that it appeared as if life, instead of wearing its sunniest aspect, had made her case an exception to the general rule, and taken away the roses of health and the buoyancy of youth, while she should have been basking in the light and glory of her third septenniad. Her health, during childhood, had been delicate, but not to any great degree. Release from school, and liberty to follow the bent of her own inclination, were expected to give her robust health and a contented mind.

But Delia soon learned that no state had ever been so irksome as that which left her mistress of her own time, and arbitress of her own destiny. Those who knew that she had a full purse, a happy home, and a circle of indulgent relatives, wondered that she should ever be melancholy. The second winter of her emancipation from the restraints imposed by her teachers, found her not only listless and dejected, but actually ill both in body and mind.

Now, as another snow-storm was evidently approaching, deferring still longer the prospect of fine weather, she sank into a large, lolling chair, and felt, to use her own expression, that she was "ready to follow the advice bestowed upon the much-enduring Job, by his impatient wife, to 'curse God and die.'"

The mother raised her hands and eyes, with a look of horror at her daughter's impiety. The father glanced furtively toward his smitten child, uttered a few soothing words, and again relapsed into silence. Ella, an impulsive girl of fourteen, lost all her smiles and dimples. James, a year older, but decidedly her inferior, looked up in blank amazement. Carrie, a little elf, not yet numbering her fifth year, pleaded with her ruby lips for a kiss, as she said, in plaintive accents, "Dear Delia."

The door opened. Charles, the eldest son, a young man of twenty-four, entered, accompanied by his betrothed, Adelaide Wilmot. Ella clapped her hands, shouting—

"You are welcome. We are all as dull as Delia, who has been talking of death, as if that were an idea for young people."

"Ella, Ella," remonstrated Mrs. Thornton, "when will you remember what I have so often told you— that the young die as well as the old?"

"I remember it, mamma, as well as my alphabet; but I believe, with Adelaide, that I may live my threescore years and ten, if I obey the laws which God has given for the preservation of life and health."

"Come, come, child," interposed her father, "you are quite too young to talk in that way. Take your book, and learn your lesson."

Ella obeyed, with a sigh; for, although an eager student, she would gladly have participated in the conversation.

Meanwhile, Adelaide, having taken a seat near Delia, was kindly inquiring for her health, but with a countenance too cheerful to imply much sympathy with the young invalid's distress.

Delia, turning away, with a petulant air, muttered, "You need not ask. You know that I am never well."

Charles, who was sitting opposite, silently watching the progress of the interview, colored at Delia's rudeness. He looked intently upon the future sisters-in-law, and sadly suspected that no congeniality of sentiment would ever be manifested.

Adelaide was a noble specimen of womanhood;

a perfect contrast to the fragile being who sat by her side. Delia was pale, slender, and low-spirited; a fair representative of thousands of American girls. Adelaide had a well-rounded, symmetrical figure, eyes beaming with health and gayety, and cheeks tinged with the brilliant hues of the carnation. Thought kindled upon her lofty brow, and hope irradiated her expressive countenance.

"How could you venture out in such a storm?" asked Delia, wearily, as if a sense of the civility due to her guest was prevailing over her unsocial feelings.

"Oh," answered the visitor, with a bright smile, "I enjoy a storm. I triumph in overcoming the obstacles presented by the raging elements. Therefore, I proposed to sally forth, and see for myself how pale you were, instead of sitting at home all the evening."

"Is not she a brave girl?" asked Charles, with an air of pride. "I shook a large snow-drift from her cloak into the entry. James, you can make fifty balls from the mass. As for her moccasins, they seemed three feet long, so tenaciously had the snow adhered to them."

The children laughed. Even Delia smiled. Mrs. Thornton, however, whose hospitality did not extend to stormy evenings, hastily left the room, with an ominous frown upon her brow, and directed a domestic "to sweep away the snow-drift which Miss Wilmot had brought into the house."

"Delia," said Adelaide, kindly, "are you no better?"

"Not so well," was the laconic reply.

"You should take more exercise."

Delia answered by a look of impatience. After a pause, she constrained herself to say: "I shall be well when summer comes. Winter is destructive to one's constitution; and spring, even when warm, is ruinous in its bad effects. I presume that these are only 'spring feelings.'"

"You mistake," said Adelaide, gently; "winter, in this latitude, is invigorating. From a dread of the cold, people immure themselves in their houses, sit all day by a great fire, neglect air and exercise, and eat as much as if they were laboring ten hours out of the twenty-four. In the spring, the season for the renewal of life and joy, they complain of ill health and low spirits. If the laws of life and health were obeyed during the winter, an accession of vigor would characterize the spring. Like the plants and the lower animals, human beings would display a revival of elasticity. Such are the views of an eminent physiologist."

Without being quite conscious of the act, Delia slightly moved her chair, that she might be rather more remote from the philosophic young lady. For a moment, Adelaide's countenance was shaded. She soon rallied. Then, after sporting a while with the children, and learning that Georgie was asleep in his cradle, she signified to Charles that it was time for her to return home. The light-hearted pair again went forth to encounter the storm. The children felt that all the brightness and beauty of the evening had vanished. James and Ella conned their lessons in silence. Carrie tried in vain to fashion her doll's dress in imitation of Adelaide's. The young invalid languidly rose to retire for the night.

"Delia, my darling," said her father, obstructing her passage from the room, "to-morrow you must have a physician."

A tear trickled down the pallid cheek of the young girl. She mournfully shook her head, and slowly retreated to her chamber. Her mother soon followed, to administer a dose of valerian.

II.

ELLA.

"But, upon thy youthful forehead
    Something like a shadow lies;
    And a serious soul is looking
    From thy earnest eyes."—WHITTIER.

THE next morning, Delia was commanded to prepare for a visit from the family physician. The
mandate was received with apparent indifference.
But, had the truth been known, the young lady
actually rejoiced. She knew that, once under the
care of a medical practitioner, she should be comparatively free from the opinions of well-meaning
but officious friends, who were constantly prescribing adverse plans of treatment. These, however
good in some particular cases, were about as ineffi-
cient for the relief of " all the ills that flesh is heir
to," as the various patent medicines trumpeted
through the world by empirics.

As Ella was preparing for school, Mr. Thornton
directed her to call, as she went, upon Dr. Perry,
and request his attendance.

Little Carrie raised her eyes, and said, " Ella
does all the errands. Why don't you send Jamie ?"

"Because, my pet, Jamie is a shy lad, and I can not bear to torture him. Ella should have been a boy, for she has all the boldness and hardihood which ought to have fallen to the lot of her brother. She shall do the boy's work, and Jamie may stay with his mamma."

Poor, bashful James blushed with pain and mortification, while Ella sagely shook her head, saying, in a low tone, "I have no objection. I will now do boy's work. Ten years hence, I will do man's work. I will now collect bills, deliver messages, and cast partial payments for my father. By-and-by, I will go through the country, lecturing on the rights of my sex. The women have more power now than the men. With equal privileges, they would rise far higher."

"Ella, Ella," called her mother, "what absurd nonsense are you muttering?"

But Ella had gone. Her father watched her from the window as long as her sturdy little figure continued visible. The child proceeded rapidly, and with an energy which might have satisfied even Dr. Franklin. The philosopher would have acknowledged that she indeed walked as if she had an object in view.

The father resumed his seat for a few moments before going to his counting-room. James, with a humiliating consciousness of his insignificance, and a groan as he thought of his unfinished lessons, crept timidly to school. Carrie, engaged in the absorbing occupation of fabricating a lilac-colored silk bonnet for her doll to wear during the ensuing summer. Charles opened his writing-desk, and arranged thereupon pen and paper, with the laudable intention of writing an elegant essay, which he hoped to be invited to deliver before some literary society. Delia reclined in the lolling chair, and gazed vacantly upon the ceiling. The parents alternately looked at each other and at their invalid daughter.

"Delia," observed the father, "I wish that you were as well as Ella."

"Delia was never so strong as Ella," interposed the mother; "but she was as well at her age."

"Heaven preserve the health of Ella!" ejaculated the father; "but she is a strange child, not at all like a girl."

Mrs. Thornton, as if her ideas of propriety were outraged by the thought of Ella's peculiar habits, assumed her most rigid look, and exclaimed: "Ella does not satisfy me. She is too masculine; too independent. She will never be married."

"Then, my dear wife, we shall always have the pleasure of her society. I should be truly sorry to give away my darling Ella."

The mother looked lovingly upon her drooping, dejected Delia, and remarked: "I dislike to see a girl with Ella's habits of thought and expression. A woman should be a true woman, exhibiting the grace and beauty of the feminine character. Not a doubtful kind of being, reminding you now of one sex, and now of the other."

She paused, and glanced toward Charles. Perceiving that he was evidently lost in thought, she continued: "Ella is too much like Adelaide."

Charles abruptly rose from his writing, and with the remark, "You could not give your daughter a greater compliment, madam," retired to the solitude of his own room.

At that moment Ella rushed into the house, her mouth open, her eyes starting, and her hair disheveled.

"What is the matter, Ella?" asked her mother, half angrily; "I did hope that I should not again see you till eleven o'clock."

"I forgot my theme, mamma."

While Ella was searching for the missing document, her father asked, "Did you deliver my message?"

"Yes, papa; and the doctor promised to come in the course of the morning. O, dear, I shall certainly be tardy!"

"If you are, you will be justly punished for your carelessness," remarked her mother.

"Ah, here it is!" and the eager girl was darting from the room, when her mother stopped her, saying, "Ella Thornton, you shall not go in that plight. Tie your shoes, and sew on your bonnet string."

Ella silently obeyed, but with a portentous frown upon her brow.

"There, now you may go, and do try to keep your mouth closed. You look as if you were going to harangue all whom you meet."

"I can't help it, mamma. My upper lip is so short, that if I close my mouth my chin will be completely puckered. But I don't care. It proves that I shall be an orator. Then I have another sign. I was born on the ninth day of the month. The ninth verse of the thirty-first chapter of Proverbs is, 'Open thy mouth, judge righteously, and plead the cause of the poor and needy.' My destiny is marked. I shall open my mouth, not only for those who are physically poor and needy, but for the countless multitudes who are mentally oppressed and indigent."

In her ardor, the child forgot the danger of delay in reaching school. She stood with her eyes dilating, and her chest heaving with emotion. Her mother was silent, with half-suppressed rage. Her father's countenance expressed triumph slightly tinged with displeasure. Ella looked fondly upon her paper.

"What is the subject of your theme, Ella?"

The little girl raised her eyes, and joyously answered, "'The Female Lecturers of the Present Day.' Miss Adams said that we must all take sides, either for or against the practice of public speaking by women. The school is divided into two sections. We rank ourselves as we please with regard to the discussions."

"Which side have you taken?"

"That it is not only right and proper, but very desirable that women should speak in public."

Without a word, Mrs. Thornton seized the theme, and threw it among the blazing coals. Mr. Thornton started with an expression of regret. Ella uttered one cry of anguish, and then, with quivering lip, wended her way to school. As the father watched the now sorrowful figure of his child, he observed—

"I am sorry, my dear wife, that you burned Ella's theme. I never before saw so much misery depicted upon her young face. It will haunt me through the day."

"Mr. Thornton, I am surprised that you should agree with that perverse girl. She is a constant source of trouble. I do wish that you would send her to boarding-school."

"What, send away my darling Ella! I could not live without her. As for her Quixotism, it will vanish in a few years. All this froth and foam will disappear. The talent and originality will remain. I shall be proud of my child. I am sure that she will gain renown."

"That is what I should not wish for any daughter of mine. Ella must leave home. She is beyond my control."

"I will take charge of her. Ask me any other favor. If you wish, I will send away all the rest.

I must have Ella by my side.   Poor child!   I wish that you had not burned her theme."

Mrs. Thornton's aspect was now so decidedly Xantippian, that her terrified husband hastily made preparations for departure.   As he held the door in his hand, he could not refrain from saying—

"Of one thing, I am certain.   The minds of both Ella and Adelaide will be occupied with subjects of so high an order, that, in conversing with them, their husbands will never have occasion to quote Solomon's declaration, 'It is better to dwell in the wilderness, than with a contentious and an angry woman.' "

III.

ALLOPATHY.

"A wild and weary life is thine;
A wasting task and lone."—MRS. HEMANS.

DR. PERRY was a physician of the old school, a genuine allopathist. He regarded with sovereign contempt the various modern systems, declaring that the whole human race would gradually degenerate, if people continued to employ young gentlemen, who thought themselves wiser than even Galen himself, and who believed that because a few cures had been apparently wrought by cold water or "clam-shell and sugar," that all the old practitioners should retire from the profession, and leave the field open and undisturbed for the trial of their experiments. For many years the large and flourishing village of Clinton had been the undisputed province of Dr. Perry. No brother M. D. had ventured to interfere. But, within a few months, the "Clinton Chronicle" had presumed to insert in its columns an advertisement purporting that Dr. Liston, a regular physician of the homeopathic order, recently arrived from erudite Germany—that land of students and philosophers—had taken rooms at

the house of the Widow Stipend, and that he would
be happy to respond to the calls of the afflicted.
The wicked little newspaper had also consented to
notify the public, that Dr. Seymour, a pupil of the
renowned Priessnitz, of Graefenburg, was practicing
in the metropolis ; that he had hired a large, com-
modious dwelling; that he was ready to receive
patients from all parts of the country, and drench
them in the most approved manner.   Dr. Perry
called upon the erring editor, and, with great solemnity, assured him that if he persisted in publishing advertisements of that character, he would
certainly be responsible for the lives of his fellow-
men.   The editor humbly replied, that being totally
ignorant of medicine, he could not be censured for
making known the claims of the various professors,
that he had established his press for the especial
purpose of enlightening the public mind, and that
he should not fulfill his obligations if he did not
print every thing which might possibly benefit the
people.   He added, moreover, that the homeopathists had cured his wife of an indescribable malady
which had afflicted her for years.   In gratitude,
therefore, he would oblige the man of pillules and
powderettes to the end of his life.   With an inimi-
table look of disdain, Dr. Perry demanded his bill,
and ordered that his name should be erased from
the list of subscribers to the " Clinton Chronicle."
As the veteran retreated, the independent editor
exchanged smiles with his printers, saying, "That

man looks more like a pirate than a physician. I would not trust my life in his hands."

Meantime, Dr. Perry, little thinking that he had been compared to a lawless prowler upon the ocean, gravely proceeded toward the residence of the Thorntons. His appearance was certainly unprepossessing. He had a tall, gaunt figure, surmounted by an enormous head of shaggy, black hair, which, in front, shaded features of a remarkably saturnine cast; and, in the rear, fell upon shoulders massive enough to undertake the labors of Hercules. Entering the house, he unceremoniously inquired for the patient. He evidently expected a serious case of fever, cholera, or, at least, measles or whooping-cough. Receiving no reply from the mistress of the house, who was sitting in a very sentimental attitude, with a perfumed handkerchief at her eyes, he carefully modulated his voice, and asked, "My dear madam, what is the matter? Who is ill? How do you do, Delia? You are as fair as a lily. As for my little Carrie, I am quite sure that she is in perfect health. Where is the patient?"

"Oh, doctor," sighed Mrs. Thornton, amazed that the physician's penetration had failed to read indications of fearful disease upon the countenance of her eldest daughter, "Delia's health has been declining for several months;" then lowering her voice to a whisper, which was, however, perfectly audible to the young lady, "I am afraid that she is in a consumption."

"Nonsense, madam," was the courteous reply of the physician, while he scrutinized the invalid with rather a fiend-like expression of countenance.

Oh, these doctors! Give them a patient actually ill in bed, racked with pain, tossed with fever, or raving with delirium, and they are enraptured. They have a fair subject for the exercise of their professional skill, and they complacently anticipate a series of highly entertaining experiments upon their unconscious victim. But, to be summoned to prescribe for a nervous young lady, with no particular disease, who has, or fancies that she has, a thousand contradictory symptoms, would almost extort an expression of impatience from the very mildest of the faculty.

After one sigh of submission, Dr. Perry assumed a tone of raillery.

"Well, Delia, let us try to exorcise your evil spirit. How do you feel? What are your symptoms?"

Delia, who could hardly conceal her aversion to the physician, replied, with downcast eyes and languid tones, "My head aches. My food distresses me. I have no strength. I often have palpitations of the heart."

"Yes, doctor," interposed Mrs. Thornton, with great solemnity, "we are afraid that she has some disease of the heart."

"None at all, madam; her palpitations are the result of indigestion, caused by want of exercise, or the use of improper articles of diet. Give me your hand, Delia. If you think that you are sick, I must examine your pulse."

Delia extended her hand, very much in the manner of a child doomed to the ferule.

"Now, Delia, if I were a school-master," laughed the physician, " but I want the wrist, not the palm of your hand."

With professional skill, he immediately placed his finger upon the desired artery. He smiled as he concluded this examination, and said: " Now I will look at your tongue."

Delia slowly protruded the summoned member. Dr. Perry again smiled. Taking pencil and paper from his pocket, he quietly wrote a prescription. Then, rising abruptly, he said : "I must now go, for I promised to call at ten o'clock upon a lady, who, because she has two or three decayed teeth which need extracting, imagines that she is tortured by neuralgia. I intend to make her submit to the application of cold iron. In the afternoon, Delia, I will bring my stethoscope, merely to convince you that your heart is not affected. I am already satisfied that you are in no danger. Take the medicine which I have ordered, walk five or six miles every day, and you will soon be perfectly well."

Dr. Perry now rushed from the house, leaving his patient in tears, and her mother in a violent paroxysm of rage. The dinner-hour had never been so eagerly expected. It came, and with it Mr.

Thornton and the other wanderers. Charles had brought Adelaide, that she might immediately learn the result of the physician's visit.

" What is the matter ? Is my sister really ill ?" asked the young gentleman, as he observed his mother's ominous brow.

Mr. Thornton's expression was solicitous, but he carefully restrained himself, knowing, by the experience of many years, that any indication of impatience only deferred still longer the gratification of his wishes.

Mrs. Thornton began : " To think that Dr. Perry, whom we have patronized ever since our marriage—" here the lady became slightly hysterical, and her auditors summoned all their forbearance—" to think that after paying him so much money for medical attendance, he should have treated us in this way !"

Her husband begged an explanation. Without needing him, she resumed her tirade.

" Dr. Perry has always been promptly paid. We have had enormous bills. One case of rheumatism, two of typhoid fever, three of throat distemper, four of cholera infantum, and five of jaundice. Eight teeth extracted for you and myself, and sixty-seven for the children. Three sprained ankles, and one broken arm—"

" My dear wife," implored Mr. Thornton, whose appetite for his dinner was not much improved by these details, " pray, tell me, without further preamble, why you are so excited."

"Why, Dr. Perry has had the impudence to say that nothing is the matter with Delia."

The gentleman's countenance cleared. "We ought to be truly grateful. I can not imagine why you are so angry."

"Mr. Thornton," enunciated the lady, with great dignity, "if Dr. Perry were infallible, I should be very far from angry. I know that Delia is actually ill."

"Let me see the recipe."

A strip of paper was produced, revealing characters almost hieroglyphic in appearance. Mr. Thornton surveyed the writing with a puzzled air. Charles followed his example.

"Adelaide," asked the young gentleman, "can not you be the Champollion to decipher these symbols?"

After one glimpse of the paper, Adelaide answered, with a half-suppressed smile, "Quinine is the medicine ordered."

"So, Delia," shouted Ella, "you are to take quinine, that wonderful medicine, which, if we may credit the statements of Mrs. Kirkland, is called 'Queen Ann' at the West."

"Be quiet, Ella, dear," said Charles. "Adelaide, can you tell us why Dr. Perry has written for quinine?"

"He evidently wishes to give her some curable form of disease. He can effect nothing by trying directly to banish the indescribable ailments that now bear sway. By introducing some disorder which he can cure, he is doubtless confident that she will soon be relieved."

If the color of Mrs. Thornton's cheeks had before indicated some degree of emotion, the now rapidly deepening hue revealed that yet undeveloped susceptibilities could be aroused. With all her dislike for Adelaide, she had a profound respect for the young lady's talents and erudition.

"What!" she ejaculated, "Dr. Perry actually intends to make Delia sick! A fine way to cure her! A beautiful expedient for running up a bill! The murderer! the extortioner!"

"My dear madam," exclaimed Adelaide, as Mrs. Thornton laid threatening hands upon the recipe, "very good reasons may be given for Dr. Perry's intended plan of treatment. Excuse me, but you have never bestowed much attention upon the subject of medicine."

But Mrs. Thornton's wrath was not to be appeased. The paper, torn into a thousand fragments, was thrown upon the glowing anthracite. Many a sacrifice had been made upon this domestic altar. Ella's theme and Dr. Perry's recipe were not the only burnt-offerings which had been thus consumed!

IV.

TABLEAUX.

"Rêves d'amour, de gloire,
D'amitié !
Rendez-moi leur mémoire,
Par pitié !
Je tâcherai d'en croire
La moitié."—NODIER.

My reader, that you may become better acquainted with the characters of this narrative, you may now attend to the examination of a series of tableaux, which shall be faithfully explained and illustrated by the exhibiter.

SCENE FIRST. *The Hour of Twilight.*

Mr. Thornton is sitting in his counting-room, ostensibly engaged in inspecting a ledger just presented for approval by his book-keeper. The gentleman does not at all resemble a merchant, but it is in that character that he is known by the assessors. *Merchant* is also printed against his name in the pages of the "Clinton Directory." Comparatively small as the town may be considered, it has actually begun to boast of a directory, that all the inhabitants may have an opportunity of obtaining

that kind of information so imperatively demanded
by a people of business habits. Mr. Thornton is
nearly three-score years of age, but his hair, although thinned by the relentless scythe of the
mower, can not yet receive the epithet of silvery.
It still retains the rich brown hue that it wore in
early manhood. His brow is almost entirely devoid
of furrows, and his face even now glows with as
ruddy a tinge as when, about forty years since, he
commenced an extended career of mercantile transactions. I say *as* ruddy, which does not, however, imply that his complexion was ever highly
colored. No; the tint was very far from that of
the ripe mountain fruit; for, even in his youth,
the blood flowed languidly through his veins. His
temperament was decidedly lymphatic. His parents
committed a serious error when they sent him to
the counting-room. His was not the brain for
mighty plans, by which the treasures of all climes
should be triumphantly conveyed into his own
store-houses. Commerce never derived much advantage from his speculations, if, indeed, by this
term of complex import, his petty schemes could
be dignified. He never enriched either his country
or himself by gigantic efforts for the introduction
of new articles of trade, or by expedients for the
skillful importation of such as were already in demand. But, although never ranking with the sons
of opulence, he towered far above the children of
penury. His mercantile affairs were intrusted to a

careful accountant; and his domestic polity had a most watchful superintendent, in the person of the active, resolute woman to whom, in a good hour for his financial concerns, but in an evil one for his home comfort, he had plighted irrevocable vows. Mr. Thornton is tenderly loved by his children, who take pleasure in contrasting their father's indulgent mood with their mother's captious, vigilant demeanor. Being indolent himself, he is always dependent on others for entertainment. Apparently half asleep, he will sit hour after hour, listening to Delia's musical performances, or to Ella's sprightly conversation. Nothing pleases him better than to hear Ella's clear, youthful voice, giving utterance to the vigorous thought and sportive fancy which, even at this early age, rivet the attention of the auditor. Although too slothful ever to bestow more care than is absolutely requisite upon his business transactions, and too great a lover of his ease to think of aspiring to the honors of a popular orator, he experiences much gratification by giving heed to the fully developed powers of others. He attends lectures and debates, listens to sermons and discussions, lends an unwearying ear to the conversation of his friends, but seldom arouses himself from his torpor to make one effort of his own. Ella is his favorite child; he sees that she has great mental power, and he will be the last to make objection, should she, a few years hence, rank as author, lecturer, or even should she assume a professor's chair. He would enjoy renown, but would prefer that, in his case, it should be reflective. Were the building in which he is sitting on fire, or were he pursued by the freed occupants of a menagerie, he would not be greatly terrified, nor would he make any violent, indecorous exertions for flight. He would resign himself to danger with the calm sentiment of the Mohammedan, "Allah wills it." His submission would not be a token of his piety, but an exponent of the utter listlessness and apathy which have characterized him even from the days of boyhood.

Scene Second. *Morning.*

Mrs. Thornton, arrayed in a dingy cap, a faded chintz wrapper, and a ragged check apron, is ensconced at a small table, occupying a conspicuous position in the basement story. Her husband has, more than once, humbly suggested that the cost of a neat suit for household labor would be very trifling, but the parsimonious lady cares neither for pleasing the eye of the beholder, nor for bestowing part-worn clothes upon poor relatives or "fragment societies." She therefore persists in rendering her personal appearance quite hideous the first few hours of the day. With no very kindly glance, she is now surveying the operations of her domestics. The elder, a rosy damsel, from that indefinite portion of territory called "Down East," has no capacity, as Mrs. Thornton has frequently averred, for learning to compound pies and tarts in the most approved manner. She is now making a fresh attempt under the scrutinizing eye of her mistress. The younger, a pale, weary girl, recently arrived from " green Erin," is vainly striving to pare apples, without committing the enormity, every day laid to her charge, of abstracting a third part of the fruit, in her efforts to separate the skin from the pulp. Mrs. Thornton is engaged in the laudable task of giving lessons in the culinary art. Well, it is yet early morning. No objection can reasonably be made to the lady's presence in her own kitchen, but the spectator longs to entreat that she would be rather more sparing in the use of invective. But enchained as she is by the habits of forty-five years in this world of rivet and cement, it would now be almost impossible that she should ever give evidence of possessing a "meek and quiet spirit." In her own view, she has experienced bitter trials. After a youth of comparative ease, she married a man unable to cope with the difficulties of life. Naturally violent in temper, with a heart uncontrolled by lofty principle, and a mind unfertilized by the dews of knowledge, she has become irritable as well as passionate. Assuming the lead, she is the real, while her husband contents himself with the position of nominal head of the family. The two are an apt representation of the mild Tarquinius and the ferocious Tullia. If the consequences of murder were now as light as in the early days

of the seven-hilled city, it is quite possible that the
result of this union would also be fatal. Mrs.
Thornton is too pharisaical ever to dream that, had
she lived in the ages that are past, prior to the
Christianizing of public sentiment, she might have
been guilty of crimes as atrocious as any that
blacken the historic page.

SCENE THIRD. *An hour after the morning session of
the "Clinton High School."*

The preceptor, who is none other than our friend
Charles, is standing, chalk in hand, before a blackboard. By his side is a boy, with sorrowful face
and drooping mien, gazing hopelessly upon the inscribed diagrams. The unfortunate lad has this
day earned the stigma of *dunce*, for he has been
unable to comprehend the test problem. Even
now, with the assistance of his teacher, he can
not cross the "*Pontem Asinorum*." His class-
mates, six girls and three boys, have all succeeded
in mastering this problem—dreaded, but simple
and beautiful in the eyes of all those who are not
wholly devoid of mathematical talent. Unhappy
William declares, with quivering lip, that he can
not understand geometry, and earnestly begs that
he may be allowed to discontinue the study. The
teacher sighs, dismisses the boy, and then, exhausted, sinks into his chair, and supports his aching
head with his hand. Despair not, friend, thy pupil
is not dull, deficient though he may be in love for

the exact sciences, and even of ability for initiation
into their mysteries. Thou art often enraptured
with glimpses of his brilliant fancy. Forms of
beauty in the changing clouds, the myriadic host
of stars, and even in the thronged city, are all carefully noted and well appreciated by this boy of intellect so apparently obtuse. A few years hence,
his beautiful imaginings will delight the world.
As yet, oh, patient teacher, thou dost not see the
glory that will gild his path! The fate of thine
other pupils is also vailed by obscurity. As thine
eye falls upon the rough boy or the heedless girl,
thou canst not discern the transformation which a
few years will reveal of the careful mechanic, the
notable housewife. That merry little girl, so generous to all, and so facile of comprehension, instead
of being the light and joy of an American home,
will cross the ocean to impart a knowledge of the
living God to the adorers of the inanimate. The
exuberance of her spirits will be modified. A most
beautiful serenity will succeed. Not the calm
which results from mental inaction, but that which
arises from the perfect harmony of all the powers.
Exhibiting, in her own character, the beauty of our
holy religion, she will win as many hearts by her
exemplification of the precepts of the gospel, as by
her regular ministrations of its truths. Thou shalt
assuredly reform the boy whose early inclination
for evil so alarms thy soul. Pure in heart, and of
spotless reputation, he shall take thine own place,

and endeavor to lead the young in the path marked
for him by his own teacher.   That girl, of undoubt-
ed talent, but of indolent habits, will, in consequence of thy efforts, become studious and method-
ical.   In attainments, she will, at no very distant
day, equal Olympia Morata herself.   She may, perchance, declaim in Greek and Latin.   She will
certainly possess the power.   Only a few of thy
present pupils will be distinguished.   But all will
be good citizens.   Thou hast been head of this
school but one week.   Thou art now almost dis-
couraged by the hopeless aspect of thy charge.   Be
not driven from the field.   Thou hast not mistaken
thy vocation.   Go on, and fulfill thy destiny.

SCENE FOURTH.   *Ten in the Morning.*

The parlor of a neat little brown cottage, a mile
distant from the mansion of the Thorntons.   The
windows are draped with linen hangings, of a refreshing green hue; for in that room, through all
the long hours of the weary day, reclines an invalid,
whose eyes can hardly bear even the softened light.
The bed is curtained, but not so as to exclude the air.
On it reposes an elderly man, with no hope of ever
again rising and walking forth upon the glad earth.
This is Adelaide's father.   A painful chronic malady has crippled his limbs, distorted his frame, and,
at times, almost deprived him of reason.   With no
hope of relief, and no prospect of recovery, chained
to his couch, like a condemned man to his cell, he

blesses God for the gift of his children. He was formerly a mariner. Eight years since, he returned from his last voyage, with a constitution broken by exposure, and a heart heavy with the thought that he could no more sail upon the mighty deep. Sadly did he alight from the carriage which had borne him from the ship to his cottage home. There, new grief was awaiting him. His beloved wife, who had always wept the departure of her ocean lord, and joyously greeted his return, had gone to the land where there is " no more death, neither sorrow, nor crying." The motherless girls clung, weeping, to their bereaved father. The wretched man groaned in agony of spirit Adelaide was then a blushing girl of sixteen; Rose, a fairy child of nine. The record of that evening was—They sat down and wept, and none strove to comfort them. The next morning, the young Adelaide, upon whom all now depended, arose long before day, resolutely banished every thought of her own grief, and seriously pondered upon the wisest course to be pursued. A physician was early summoned to pronounce upon her father's case. The result was far from encouraging. He could give no hope of cure, and but very little of relief. Life might continue many years, but the tenure would be held on very hard terms. Racking pain would henceforth be his frequent attendant. During her childhood, Adelaide's energy had been uncommon; now it became absolutely indomitable. While she sorrowed for her

father, she endeavored to wear a cheerful countenance, that no new misery might be inflicted upon
the unhappy man. She gently asked for a strict
account of the state of his pecuniary affairs. All his
papers were submitted to her inspection. She saw
that the amount of property was the smallest possible that could be honored by the name of an independence. She dismissed the teacher with whom
she was reading French and Latin, congratulating
herself that the already advanced stage of her progress would enable her to pursue her studies without assistance. She withdrew Rose from school,
knowing that she should need her aid at home,
and that the child could study under her super-
vision, without taking half the time usually expend-
ed by those under the care of a teacher with thirty
pupils. She discharged the domestic, being certain
that she could afford no extra expense. Adelaide's
mind was of such an order, that circumstances over-
whelming to others, served only as agreeable stimulants for the exercise of her powers. Despite her
distress, she experienced actual pleasure in obviating the numerous difficulties of her position. Convinced that a life of labor was before her, she submitted, with only one longing, retrospective glance
toward the dreaming days of her childhood. She
would, henceforth, be the nurse, housekeeper, and
companion of her father; the guide, teacher, and
playmate of her sister. She looked abroad into the
world, wishing that she could do something to in-

crease their limited income. This being impossible, while her father required so much of her time, she resolutely abandoned the idea. Indeed, she soon found that almost every hour had its work. The main part of the household labor devolved upon her. In addition to this, she carefully cultivated the land attached to the cottage, and smiled as she thought, that besides pleasing the eye with her flowers and shrubbery, she was also saving several dollars every year, by raising all the fruit and vegetables desirable for the supply of their table. As very little money entered the house, she knew that the expenses must be proportionately small. At the end of the first year, she found that the debt and the credit side of the account exactly balanced. While she rejoiced that they were thus independent of the world, she sighed as she thought of the strict economy requisite for the maintenance of the freedom. This mode of life continued for several years. She, every day, found a little time for the prosecution of her own studies. The education of Rose was never neglected. Thus, she gradually became, both in body and mind, the strong, fearless woman, qualified for the performance of any needful labor or the endurance of any requisite sacrifice. About three years before the commencement of my story, she had formed an acquaintance with the publisher of one of the most popular magazines of the day. By him she had been induced to write for its pages. The remuneration, although small, was sufficient,

in her circumstances, to encourage further effort.
She still continued her course of labor and economy.
The additional money gained enabled her to think
of the desirable as well as the indispensable; to extend the hand of relief to those beyond as well as
those within the circle of her own immediate household. It is in the exercise of her new vocation that
you this morning see her. As the father reposes
upon his couch of pain, and the youthful Rose cons
a self-imposed lesson, Adelaide sits musingly at a
little pine table, and embodies those airy "beings
of the mind," whose ideal beauty constitutes so
large a portion of the happiness of those favored by
their presence. She is truly "coining her brain into
drachmas," if I may be allowed slightly to vary the
phraseology of the immortal dramatist. Leave her
now, amid the bright scenes conjured by her imagination, and the beauteous habitants of the fairy
world, and glance at a picture in which the shade
far exceeds the glow.

SCENE FIFTH. *Ten in the Morning.*

The clock strikes, and Delia, as she counts the
notes, endeavors to summon courage to arise. She
is actually well enough to be abroad in the fields,
as soon as Aurora throws aside her vail, and raises
her rose-tinged fingers to unclose the portals of day.

Delia is a young lady sadly deficient in regular
habits. Occasionally she exerts herself to rise at
dawn; then again relapsing, she is not visible be-

yond the precincts of her chamber, till the sun is
rapidly approaching the zenith. She is always
forming good resolutions, which only need accomplishment to convince the world of the wisdom of
their designer. She is a true ivy, ever clinging to
some friendly prop for support and countenance.
In any emergency, she would prefer that her friends
should decide for her, rather than evoke her own
powers for independent thought and action. Were
she poor, she would never seek a free maintenance
by her own exertions, but would look for the aid of
relatives or charitable societies. Her great want is
an object in life. Were this supplied, she might
possibly become an estimable member of the community. This might arouse her latent energy, and
indirectly vanquish the obstacles which now interpose to prevent her from standing alone in the
world, and taking upon herself some plan of life
that would enable her to be independent of others.

SCENE SIXTH. *Sabbath Morning.*

The bells are ringing. James, having timidly
advanced through the main street, is nervously
standing upon the threshold of the church. He is
surveying, with looks of trepidation, his unfortunate
feet, this day encased in a pair of new shoes. He
is dreading to walk the uncarpeted aisle, with his
feet thus formidably enveloped. He knows that
the major part of the people, not being devotionally
inclined, will turn their heads as soon as the first

creak of his new shoes shall greet their sensitive
ears. James is always thus suffering. He is one
of those people who, as has wittily been suggested,
beg pardon of the world for their intrusion. I suspect that James, with all his apparent humility,
with all his absence of pretension, has a tinge of
vanity in his character, or he would not so often be
troubled with the vision of a thousand eyes directed
toward his insignificant little person. Be a man,
Jamie, if thou canst. It is certain, however, that
thou wilt never be a distinguished one; for thy shy-
ness is not the kind which is sometimes the attendant of genius; it is rather of that order which those
who are really devoid of power feel when in the
presence of their superiors.

SCENE SEVENTH. *The Sunset Hour.*

Ella, the wayward, the half-beautiful, the im-
passioned child, ever unyielding to aught save the
decisions of her own free will, is sitting pensively
before an open window, her waving hair lawlessly
floating over her shoulders, while her large, blue
eyes are reverently raised to behold the gorgeous
aspect of the retiring orb. Power is inscribed upon
every movement of her noble head, upon every
glance of her keen, brilliant eyes—power yet undeveloped, but revealing promise of exceeding good,
or of immeasurable evil, as it shall be hereafter directed. In early childhood, Ella was nearly as
quiet as James. Only within a year or two has the

change been wrought. "With the games of her youth," has also been left the infantile spirit of blind submission and innocent credulity, pleasing only in very early life. She has begun to think with vigor; and woe to herself and to the world if she does not learn conformity to the laws of her being!

Scene Eighth. *Noon.*

Carrie, a cherub child, with beauty reminding one of Eastern splendor, so deep and rich are its hues, is sitting upon the door-step, awaiting her father's approach. Mark the jetty hair; the clear, olive complexion, tinted with ruby; the dark eyes, startling the beholder with their luster. But the spirit of the child is very tranquil. There is something in the quiet of the old father's mood singularly attractive to his little daughter. She will sit with him hour after hour, neither asking nor desiring any active enjoyment. Will she, in after life, resemble the ivine Delia, the heroic Adelaide, or the imperial Ella? She now appears too well ever to be of the invalid order, too helpless ever to bear the responsibility of care and labor, and too serene ever to enjoy all the beauty and luxuriance of life. But she has not yet emerged from the shadows that hover around the path of infancy. She is too young for any one to predict her destiny.

Scene Ninth. *Morning.*

Georgie, a delicate little fellow, with clusters of

flaxen curls, depending from a head of unparalleled beauty, although the phrenologists have been ominously grave on witnessing the exponents of character therein indicated, is examining, with philosophic eye, some prim wooden figures, collectively styled "Noah's Ark." There is an elephant no larger than the dog barking by his side; and a beetle equal in size to the head of Mrs. Japhet, who stands with her seven relatives, meekly watching the vast caravan. It may be that the various phenomena displayed are exciting Georgie's organ of wonder, and arousing his yet dormant powers of investigation, to discover whether the animals in the days of Noah were actually so disproportionate, or whether the artisan who constructed their representatives was ignorant of the first principles of natural history. Georgie is, of course, esteemed a prodigy by the whole family. His features have been severally claimed by all the relatives. It is generally agreed that he resembles, in some respect, every individual connected with the Thorntons, even by the most remote ties of consanguinity. If the predictions daily uttered are verified, he will certainly surpass all the heroes and scholars of both ancient and modern times.

V.

HYPATIAN.

"Higher, higher will we climb
Up to the mount of glory,
That our names may live through time
In our country's story.

"Minds are of celestial birth,
Make wo then a heaven of earth."—JAMES MONTGOMERY.

At last, the mild south wind blew; the gentle rain fell in copious showers. The frost-bound earth gradually moistened; the snow melted and disappeared. Now the clouds dispersed, the trees waved lightly in the breeze, the leaf-buds began to expand, and the birds sang in the branches. "The wind-flower and the violet" raised their modest heads and greeted the field-rover. The cruciform houstonia, tinged with cerulean, looked heavenward, as if there to seek its kindred. The columbine towered proudly from the rock-summit, and raised its golden nectaries as if to receive celestial manna. The New England spring had come, with its visions of unrivaled beauty.

Ella had been Queen of the May. After the festivities, she walked home as she had been arrayed

in the woods, her bright curls surmounted by a
chaplet of flowers, and her hand bearing a scepter
wreathed with moss of a vivid green hue. Had her
mother been in the room, the child would have received a severe reprimand for coming through the
street in such a guise. Charles rose with delight.

"Why, my little sister," he almost involuntarily
exclaimed, "you are really beautiful!"

"Much obliged to you, brother," answered the
triumphant girl; "I have received the same compliment a thousand times to-day. But why did
your school not have a May party?"

"Oh, because," replied Charles, with mock gravity, "my school has the misfortune to be taught by
a gentleman. A lady is required to design any
thing so beautiful as your celebration. As I was
strolling along the edge of the woods, I casually had
a view of Miss Adams and her pupils. I began to
wonder whether I had not caught a glimpse of the
Mohammedan Paradise. I should have believed
that such was the case had more of your houris
been dark-eyed."

"If you had been Mohammed, should you have
represented the women of Heaven with dark eyes?"

"Had I been Mohammed, an Arabian sensualist,
my imagination would doubtless have reveled in
visions of the same order. As, however, I am an
individual of entirely different character, belonging
to quite another race of human beings, the dreams
with which I am favored are the reverse of those

that delighted the eyes of the impostor. But, of course, I like variety. It is far more agreeable to look at you, and then at Carrie, than it would be if you both possessed the same style of beauty."

Ella laughed. "What a flatterer is my usually wise brother, telling his young sister of her personal attractions!"

"If, my dear Ella, you were a worshiper of your fine face and figure, I should be silent upon the subject. But I know that although you gratefully acknowledge your beauty as a good gift of God, you also view it as the least of the benefactions with which He has endowed you."

For a moment Ella was silent and thoughtful. A tear trembled in her eye. With an effort she soon banished all serious thought, and said sportively, "I know your reason for preferring bright blue eyes."

"Are you quite sure that you do?"

"Adelaide is a blue-eyed maiden."

For a moment Charles looked at Ella with a comic smile wreathing his features. He then said: "You are wrong, my dear. My taste was the same before I saw Adelaide. I have two reasons. First, the expression of the light eye is more easily read than that of the dark one. Second, and chief, the same reason that I should give for choosing hair with a bright tinge. It is the characteristic of the Saxon—'the race that came upon the earth to conquer it.'"

"That is not *your* reason, Charles. I have seen it in some book."

"You have a deal of acumen, Ella, for so young a head. In mercy to the unfortunate race of authors, refrain from engaging in the occupation of a reviewer. Do you know, however, that Sir Walter Scott thought it impossible for a person who had read and written a great deal not to be occasionally guilty of unintentional plagiarism. But I intended to tell you that the reason was mine only by adoption. Can you mention the real author of the sentiment?"

"I have forgotten."

"Ah! know, then, that Charles F. Briggs has the credit of the idea. Now, I have a question to ask. I did not see Julia Mansfield in your ranks. Is not she a young lady of great taste and of fine scholarship? No disparagement to you, Miss Ella, but Julia would have been a very beautiful queen."

Ella raised her mirthful eyes.

"I will explain. Julia and I were the only candidates. The balloting took place a week before the festival. We two have always been rivals. We are almost exactly matched. Last term I gained the prizes in Latin,.history, and arithmetic; Julia, in French, chemistry, and geography. We are both close students this term. Julia avers that she will gain all the prizes. I am equally determined that I will have every one of them. I am almost confident of success."

"But what has all this to do with the May Queen?" asked Charles, with a slightly troubled countenance.

"I am explaining as fast as I can. When the votes were counted, each of us had sixteen. Was it not singular? We agreed that Miss Adams should decide. Instead of voting for either of us, she said that the one who had recited the greater number of perfect lessons this term should be queen. The record-books were examined. My merits exceeded Julia's by three. It was thus that I gained the crown. Julia was so unhappy that she refused to join in the festival. I told the girls that she resembled Themistocles, who could not sleep on account of the victories of Miltiades."

With disapproval on every lineament of his countenance, Charles replied: "That was very unkind. How should you like to have such comparisons drawn?"

"Not very well, brother."

"In future, my dear, remember the golden rule. Now, I have a suggestion to make. Why can not you two, instead of being almost at variance, follow the example of Theseus and Pirithous?"

Ella colored, and was silent a few minutes. She then frankly said, "I do not understand the allusion, brother. You remember that I am only fourteen, and that my historical studies have not yet extended so far as yours."

"My dear child, ignorance is very excusable at

your age. I should be sorry if you were like the
little boy of whom Miss Edgeworth says, 'all history was clear in his head.' How many times I
have laughed at the pretensions of Master Lewis!
I will not stop to tell you the whole story of the
heroes to whom I have adverted. You shall read
it for yourself. But I will say enough to explain
my meaning. Theseus and Pirithous had met, ex-
pecting to fight; but, being strongly impressed
with each other's noble qualities, they were mutu-
ally inspired with admiration. From this, love
arose, and they became noted for their friendship."

"Oh, they joined the 'Mutual Admiration Society!' Is that your plan for Julia and myself?"

Charles faintly smiled.

"Do not flatter each other, but let your regard
be proportionate to your merit. Then, every new
excellence developed, instead of exciting envy, will
only augment affection."

Before Ella could reply, a carriage stopped.
Delia alighted, and walked slowly up the avenue,
leaning upon her father's arm. They passed the
window at which the preceptor was sitting with his
light-hearted sister. The young man sighed. After a pause, he asked, "Ella, shall you ever be like
Delia ?"

"Like Delia!" exclaimed the indignant little
girl, "I hope not. Delia merely exists, she does
not live."

"How will you avoid such a fate?"

"By being an actor, instead of a spectator, in the great drama of life. Delia has no object of interest. She is the most indifferent person that I ever saw. She cares neither for study nor amusement."

"You are right. When you leave school, continue your studies at home, but spend several hours every day in some occupation that shall directly benefit the world. All young men in this country have some art or profession. I see not why young women should be exempt from a similar rule. I truly believe that Delia would be well if she were obliged to work for her maintenance."

"What can I do, Charles?"

"In consequence of the erroneous views entertained by many men, there are now but very few employments accessible by your sex. Your education will be a very fine one. You ought not, therefore, to engage in any occupation merely requiring mechanical skill. Mind must be the material for your labor. Teaching is a dignified and honorable profession. The greatest philosophers have been schoolmasters. Both sexes, at the present day, engage largely in this work. Would this agree with your views?"

"By no means; unless, like Aspasia, I could have such pupils as Socrates and Pericles; unless, like her, I could have grown men and women for the recipients of my instructions."

Suppressing his inclination to smile, Charles an-

swered, "The career of Aspasia was, in many respects, most admirable. You may be the fortunate
woman to follow her example in modern America.
But you do not sufficiently estimate the influence
of even a common-school teacher. In some parts
of our country, young women may be the ministers
of religion as well as the teachers of secular knowledge. I have been reading a remarkable little
book, entitled 'The Duty of American Women to
their Country.' I suspect that Miss Beecher, a woman of large heart and active brain, has the chief
merit of the authorship. I will read one or two ex-
tracts to show what you might do. In one of those
destitute villages found in all parts of the West, ' a
young lady from New England, who came out under the care of a clergyman, stationed herself to
rear up a school. She agreed to teach for a small
sum, and to *board around* with the parents of her
pupils.

"'Most of these parents were from the South,
where they were unaccustomed to the notions of
comfort and thrift which the young lady possessed.

"'She not only taught the children at school,
but, in each family where she boarded, taught
the housekeeper how to make *good yeast* and
good bread. She also taught the young women
how to cut dresses and how to braid straw for
bonnets.

"'Her instructions in the day school and in the
Sunday school, and her influence in the families,

were unbounded. No minister, however well qualified, could have wrought such favorable changes
in so short a time.

" 'In another case, known to the writer, a young
lady went into such a destitute village. There was
no church, and no minister of any sect. She taught
the children through the week, and also instituted a
Sabbath school. In this she conducted religious
worship herself. Gradually the mothers came to
attend, then the fathers, until at last she found herself in the office both of teacher and clergyman.
The last portion of her duties she resigned to a minister, who, by her instrumentality, was settled
there.'

" Could you, Ella, desire more power than these
teachers possessed? My only wish, on reading the
last anecdote, was, that the noble young woman
had retained her pastoral office. It would have
been a good precedent. By such methods, women
must evince their ability. Let no favorable opportunity be neglected."

" I agree with you, brother Charles, but I thought
that men were unwilling to allow women to occupy
stations of consequence, and that we must consequently seize every privilege that seemed desirable."

" All wise men believe that whenever God bestows
a good gift, He designs that the donee should exercise
it for the benefit of the human race. Bigoted and
narrow-minded men fear that they shall be eclipsed,

if women come upon the stage of action. These will
discuss the different spheres of the sexes, their un-
equal powers, etc. They know that although woman
has an inferior domestic position, not being the head
of the family, she possesses mental power equal to
that of their own sex; but they will not acknowledge this, while they have any plea for retaining
their low and degrading views. Women must, by
their own acts, convince men that they have the
same endowments. If the universities of the land
are not open for their admission, they should pursue
an extended course of study at home."

"Oh, Charles, ought not Adelaide to have a part
in the reform? She is highly gifted, and she has
studied so much that she must now possess great
erudition."

"Adelaide," exclaimed Charles, with deep feeling, "is qualified for any position. But she hesi-
tates with regard to taking what is not yet allowed
by public opinion. Knowing that the press is regarded by many as more effective than the pulpit,
she is well content thus to give utterance to her
thoughts. Her success in the literary world now
gives promise of eminence."

"But Adelaide writes only prose. I should wish
to be a poet."

"Why, Ella, some of the most distinguished
authors have been prose writers."

"Yes; but I always think of Sappho and her
poetry. How delighted I was when I learned that

the great Solon thought one of her poems so beautiful that he should be unwilling to die till he had learned it by heart."

"That was certainly a very great honor to her who was so deservedly styled the 'Tenth Muse.' But the thoughts, if not the words, of many prose writers, are deeply graven upon the hearts of their readers. You appear to think, Ella, that poetry is mere rhyme and meter. It has been well said that poetry consists in the thought, not in the expression. Some of the finest prose compositions in our language are true poems, and the more glorious as they are devoid of metrical and rhythmical trammels. The record of thought, in whatever style, is the noblest form of usefulness. The successful author is like the renowned Pharos of antiquity, shedding far and wide pure and beautiful rays to illumine the path of the wanderer. Now, after repeating a few lines by Lowell, who would be deemed a true poet, even if he did not clothe his ideas in so attractive a garb, I must leave you to your own reflections.

> 'It may be glorious to write
>   Thoughts that shall glad the two or three
> High souls, like those far stars that come in sight
>   Once in a century;
>
> 'But better far it is to speak
>   One simple word, which now and then
> Shall waken their free nature in the weak
>   And friendless sons of men;

'To write some earnest verse or line,
    Which, seeking not the praise of art,
Shall make a clearer faith and manhood shine
    In the untutored heart.

' He who doth this, in verse or prose,
    May be forgotten in his day,
But surely shall be crowned at last with those
    Who live and speak for aye.' "

VI.

NEGOTIATION.

"In scorn I speak not;—they are what their birth
And breeding suffer them to be "—WORDSWORTH.

NOT many days after the date of Ella's visit to
Dr. Perry, the indefatigable little girl was seen
wending her way toward the residence of his homeopathic rival. She first encountered, not the potent
professor, but the lady to whose tender mercies he
had consigned himself for board and lodging.

"Good morning, Miss Ella," cried the worthy
Mrs. Stipend. "Have you come to see my little
Sarah Jane?"

"Not this morning, Mrs. Stipend. Papa sent me
for Dr. Liston. Can I see him?"

"Of course you can; don't he board here?" was
the true Yankee answer; "but, pray, tell me who
is sick."

"My sister Delia."

"Poor young lady!" sympathized Mrs. Stipend.
"I heerd that she was quite out of health. I
thought that she looked like a ghost last Sunday,
when she was led out of meeting in a fainting fit.

The 'pathic doctor'll cure her. He's a wonderful man. He'll soon have all the practice in Clinton; but"—and here the widow lowered her voice—"how did your father dare to affront old Perry? It is an awful thing to quarrel with a doctor."

"We called upon him first, as a matter of course, but he became offended with us."

'My dear," exclaimed the widow, with as great an air of condolence as if all the Thorntons had received sentence of death, "I raly pity you. Doctors know so much. To think of their understanding all the pisons on airth! Why, I was most skeered to take a doctor to board, for fear that some day he might put pison into my tea."

Ella mentally queried whether Mrs. Stipend thought that Dr. Liston would mingle poison in her tea to avoid settling her bill; or whether she supposed that physicians were a class analogous to the Thugs of India, going through life with a regular system of murder, to be carried into execution whenever a good opportunity presented itself.

Although this was a holyday, Ella had devised employment for every hour, and feeling that she could give no more time to Mrs. Stipend's absurdities, she rather abruptly said, "You told me that I could see Dr. Liston. Where is he?"

"Why, I meant that you could see him when he came home. He's gone to old Mrs. Marston's."

"I can call again in the course of the day," replied Ella, turning to depart.

"No, no, child; he'll soon be at home. Come and wait in his reception-room. I want to talk with you."

With a sigh, Ella mechanically followed her hostess, wondering why the world contained so many vexatious persons, and thinking that Carlyle was perfectly right, when he said that "the American nation consists of eighteen millions of the greatest bores that ever annoyed the earth," and, not once reflecting that she belonged to the same condemned people, and that the distinguished censor would probably have denounced her as an intolerable little pedant, deserving no less than imprisonment in the nursery till her arrival at years of discretion.

Ella seated herself, with resignation inscribed upon every lineament of her countenance.

Mrs. Stipend began: "Now, my dear, do tell me how your ma gets along with that green Irish girl of hers that—"

A shrill voice from the lower regions here called, "*Miss* Stipend, *Miss* Stipend, the lobsters are jumping out of the kettle!"

The lady precipitated herself over the stairs. Meantime, Ella, at the door of the room in which she had been left, was demanding an explanation with almost childish terror. For some moments, she received no answer. Then Mrs. Stipend reappeared, flushed and panting.

"Oh, my dear," she breathlessly exclaimed,

"the trials of house-keeping! What a sacrifice I make of my feelings by having boarders!"

" Why do you take boarders, if you find the care of them so oppressive ?"

" Ah, Miss Ella, a lone widow must earn a living some way; but I raly believe poor Mr. Stipend would come out of his grave, if he knew what I have to suffer."

The disconsolate woman now commenced rocking with great vehemence, ever and anon wiping away the tears which were flowing with a profusion that astonished her strong-minded little guest.

Thinking to divert the mourner's attention from the contemplation of her own sorrows, and stimulated also by the feelings of a true daughter of Eve, the little girl ventured to inquire, " Will you tell me, Mrs. Stipend, the cause of your recent alarm ? I did not know that people ever had live lobsters in their houses."

Mrs. Stipend raised her hands and eyes, uttering sundry incoherent ejaculations of horror. "That comes, Miss Ella, from spending all your time over your books. Girls ought to learn housekeeping."

"I intend, madam, to become thoroughly acquainted with every branch of domestic economy, and I therefore entreat that you will immediately give me a lesson on lobsters."

"You are a queer child. Well, in the first place, you know that lobsters are alive before they are killed."

"Yes, madam," replied Ella, with a countenance, the admirably demure expression of which was comically tinged with burlesque, "I am well aware of the fact."

"Well, instead of buying them all cooked, I have 'em brought here alive, and kill 'em myself."

Ella slightly screamed.

"How do you kill them?"

"Boil 'em alive. I bought half a dozen this morning. When Martha put 'em into the hot water, the pain made 'em jump out."

Ella sat aghast. Her first thought was a resolution never again to partake of lobster. Recollecting, however, that this crustaceous animal was one of her favorite articles of food, she ingeniously reasoned that if the kettle were sufficiently deep for the immersion of the unfortunate victim, the slaughter might be effected without causing any more pain than is produced by the spearing of swine, the strangling of fowls, or the harpooning of whales. But it was a sad subject, and she was fast falling into a profound metaphysical reverie, trying to solve the intricate problem concerning the suffering of agents incapable of committing acts of either good or bad moral character, when she was aroused by Mrs. Stipend, who hastily said, "Dear, dear Miss Ella, don't look so solemn. I do it to save money. It would make a great difference if all the lobsters I buy were prepared by the fishermen."

"I should think that you would rather give a little more money than to kill the poor creatures yourself."

"I assure you, child, a poor lone widow has to contrive, as I told my boarders the other day, when they grumbled because I put pounded crackers instead of eggs into the squash pies."

Ella's lip, which, it must be confessed, had rather a scornful contour, involuntarily curled with disdain. She contrasted Adelaide's noble, generous economy, with Mrs. Stipend's mean, despicable parsimony. She longed for the appearance of Dr. Liston, that she might depart. Finally, she presumed to ask, "Will you be so kind, Mrs. Stipend, as to inform Dr. Liston that his presence is desired at Mr. Thornton's?"

"Why, yes, child, if you raly must go, but do stay and see the doctor for yourself. Come, I'll find something to entertain you."

She now drew from her pocket a letter, and said, "Of course, you remember my son Johnny."

Ella's features were contracted for a moment as she recalled the image of the awkward youth, who, sitting in a pew contiguous to her father's at church, chose to peer into her bonnet, instead of directing his attention to the sermons of the Rev. Dr. Leland. Conscious that Mrs. Stipend was endeavoring to read the expression of her countenance, she blushed deeply as she answered, "I remember him perfectly well."

"Oh," exclaimed the enraptured mother, maliciously gazing upon the crimsoned visage of her victim, "all the girls blush and smile when Johnny's name is mentioned, but don't be afeerd, my dear, you're the one; Johnny said he was going to Californy to get gold enough to marry Ella Thornton."

"Mrs. Stipend!" thundered Ella, "I would not marry your son if he were the possessor of all the gold of California." Here the infuriated little girl placed peculiar stress upon the last two vowel sounds in the mispronounced name of the famed resort of the money-seekers; "I would not marry him if he were the heir of that queen ' upon whose dominions the sun never sets' "—the energetic speaker suddenly paused, recollecting some rather sermonic discourse which she had recently held with her brother Charles, and then resumed, with unusual gentleness, "you must remember, Mrs. Stipend, that I am yet too young to think of any gentleman as a lover. If I ever marry, I shall not do so before the age of twenty-five."

"Why, child, some girls are married at sixteen. You arn't at all too young to think of the subject."

"I beg leave to differ," replied Ella, calmly. "Physiology teaches that neither man nor woman should marry till the constitution has become consolidated. By the old laws of Athens, a man was not allowed to marry before the age of thirty-five, nor a woman before the age of twenty-six. In my opinion, those were very good regulations."

"Pray don't talk like doctors and lawyers, Miss Ella."

"Well, what education can a woman have who marries at sixteen or eighteen?"

"Oh, a very good one. See how well I get along. I never looked into a lesson-book after I was fourteen, and I married at seventeen."

Ella thought that Mrs. Stipend's appearance and conversation were a practical commentary on her words, and that there was no absolute need of a formal statement of her educational deficiencies; but, believing it preposterous to try to convince her of the error of her opinions, and benevolently desirous of gratifying the fond mother's vanity, she asked, "Does your son like California?"

Mrs. Stipend's good nature instantly returned. With beaming looks she said, "You shall hear his letter, my dear."

I will spare my readers the infliction suffered by Ella, as she listened to a very commonplace epistle, abounding in so many errors, both of syntax and style, that it would have served as an admirable exercise for the emendations of a student in either of those branches of knowledge. The mother's elocution was as great a curiosity as the son's composition. The closing words of every sentence were read in a very high key, and with marked emphasis, while those which led the van were so softly uttered, that they could hardly be heard by the amused auditor. Ella's impatience gradually gave place to keen enjoyment of the ludicrous, and nearly unable to preserve her gravity, she silently listened to the performance.

"There, Miss Ella," remarked the mother, as she carefully refolded the letter, "that young gentleman'll be a fine husband for somebody"—here she nodded and simpered, while the young lady quietly enjoyed the scene.

"I've been thinking," resumed the happy mother, "that this 'ere letter ought to go into the ' Clinton Chronicle.' Don't you s'pose, my dear, that the editor 'd be charmed to 'ave it? Every thing from Californy takes, 'specially a letter like this 'ere, from a man born and edicated in Clinton. I've never seen any thing in the newspaper equal to Johnny's writing."

Ella thought that she had not, but she carefully refrained from expressing her opinion.

"Come, Miss Ella," persisted the mother, eager for some tribute of praise, " isn't it very fine ?"

Ella blushed, hesitated, and played with her gloves. She at length observed, "It certainly contains a very graphic description of San Francisco."

"Yes, my dear, that's a fact; now, as you go home, why can't you take it to the editor, and tell him that it's for the newspaper, and that it came from a young gentleman, a particular friend of yours ?"

Ella started as if she had received an electric shock.

"Impossible, madam, I can not consent."

Intimidated by Ella's manner, Mrs. Stipend did not venture to press the subject. But she soon relapsed into her patronal mood.

"Well, my dear, of course you're bashful about it; I'll go myself, and I'll take care to tell the editor that Miss Ella Thornton says it's a very—graphic—yes, that's the word—a very graphic description of San Francisco."

"Mrs. Stipend," exclaimed Ella, grasping the woman's dress in her panic, "you must not mention my name!"

"Dear, dear child, don't look so like a wild creeter. You needn't be afeerd. I won't say a word about you. I know jest how you feel. I'm going now. The paper comes out to-morrow."

Ella held her breath till her tormentor had quitted the room. Then, no longer able to repress her merriment, she leaped violently into the air, threw her arms over her head, and resembled, for the time being, a person in the transports of delirium. Had Dr. Liston entered at that moment, he would have thought her a fit subject for his experiments in behalf of the insane. Before she had entirely recovered, Mrs. Stipend re-entered, half equipped for her excursion. In lisping accents, she said, "My dear child, will you have the goodness to throw my shawl over my shoulders?"

Ella, who was remarkably independent in her personal habits, never applying to any one for as-

sistance in the completion of her toilet, unconscious-
ly smiled as she attempted to comply with the
polite request.

The shawl being adjusted, Mrs. Stipend stood
awhile before the doctor's mirror, contemplating
her appearance. Indeed, both her dress and its
arrangement were a curious exhibition. Although
professing unmitigable grief for the loss of her husband, she wore a large, open bonnet, profusely
decorated with rainbow-hued ribbon. As she always assumed great floral taste, and also profound
reverence for the trophies of art, she carried on each
side of her face, in the cavity between her hair and
her bonnet, quite a parterre of nondescript flowers
and foliage, manufactured of glazed cambric and
taffeta. A skillful botanist would have been puzzled in attempting to classify these unique speci-
mens of horticulture. She wore a kaleidoscopic
dress, disfigured by three deep flounces; and a large
scarlet shawl, with a green and yellow border.
Salmon-colored gloves, and bronze slippers, completed her extraordinary attire. She stood some
ten minutes, in mute admiration of her own taste,
turning from one side to the other, alternately directing her visual organs over each shoulder, and
making strenuous efforts to view her costume from
every position. Then, tightly clasping Johnny's
precious missive in her hand, she daintily trod the
main street of Clinton, to visit the doomed editor
of the "Chronicle."

VII.

ELASTICITY.

"When Fancy's smile
Gilding youth's scenes, and promising to bring
The curtained morrow fairer than to-day."—MRS. SIGOURNEY.

BEING left alone in the reception-room of the disciple of Hahnemann, Ella began to look around in quest of amusement or occupation. She wished that she had been admitted into his study. There she would have found books. Here, naught was at first visible, save the usual furniture of a common parlor. To her great joy, however, she soon espied a slate, evidently hanging for the express purpose of receiving orders during the absence of its proprietor. She immediately wrote, " Dr. Liston is requested to call at the residence of Mr. Thornton, No. 16 Myrtle Street."

With a feeling of relief she was quitting the room, when she was suddenly met by the physician himself. She recognized him, having had her attention directed to the foreign professor, a few days prior to the occurrence of this morning's adventures. There he stood, with his large dreamy eyes, mildly contemplating the buoyant aspect of his visitor. The little girl courtsied. The gentleman bowed.

"I have called, sir," began Ella, "to ask you to attend my sister, whose health is not good. My father's name is Joseph Thornton."

The elegant stranger regarded her in silence. Surprised at his apparent abstraction, she earnestly repeated her message.

"Yes, my child," he now replied, with the pure English accent, but with the deliberation of a man not yet sufficiently familiar with the language, to express his thoughts with ease and fluency, "wait a few moments, and I will accompany you."

Ella watched the movements of her proposed escort, as he slowly unlocked his desk, calmly arranged his writing implements, and very carefully—with the air of a man engaged in scientific composition, and quite uncertain of the correctness of his views— penned a few lines in cipher. Then, withdrawing to his sanctum, he presently returned with a wallet of moderate size, opened it in his quiet manner, inspected two or three rows of tiny inch-length vials, secured in their places by kid fastenings, and containing pills resembling very small pin heads, made of some chalky substance; readjusted this very convenient pharmaceutical apparatus, deposited it in his coat pocket, and signified that he was now at liberty to go with his messenger.

The twain left the house, the physician occasionally giving his young companion so inquisitorial a

glance, that she began to wonder whether he suspected her of robbing the reception-room during
his absence.   Her doubts were soon relieved.

"My child," he said, with benignant tone, "in
personal appearance you very much resemble my
little sister, whom I left last year in Weimar."

"In Weimar," rapturously repeated Ella, "oh,
how I should like to be there with your sister!
Does she visit that beautiful library every day, and
is she acquainted with any of the great authors,
who reside in that celebrated place?"

Doctor Liston smiled as he gently answered in
the negative.   After a pause, he remarked, "The
fame of my native town has then reached you."

"Oh, yes," replied Ella, complacently, "Weimar
is called the Athens of Germany; and Boston, the
Athens of America."

A half smile flitted across the countenance of the
German as he responded to the beaming expression
of the little school girl.   During the remainder of
the walk, he made quite a companion of the delighted Ella, who, overjoyed that she had so good
an auditor, conversed with great freedom and volu-
bility, especially expatiating upon the point that
the young ladies of Germany ought to receive a
more thorough education, and declaring that the
men were very selfish in monopolizing so large a
share of the immense literary advantages enjoyed
by students in that country.

Ella and the physician were met at the door by

Mrs. Thornton, who, from the window, had been observing, with blank amazement, their apparent familiarity. She gave Ella an ominous frown, the precursor, as the child well knew, of a heavy penalty for presuming to converse with a stranger.

Dr. Liston, having been informed that Delia was the patient, commenced a more formidable list of interrogatories than had ever before been propounded to the young lady. Producing pencil and note-book, he carefully recorded all her answers. Her exact age was first marked; then the peculiarities of her constitution, as they had been revealed from birth to the present time, were elicited. An account of her habits of life was also demanded. The homeopathist was evidently a close observer. He noticed, with a critical eye, the configuration of the head, and the general physical organization of his patient. Then, the kinds of food that best suited her palate were discussed, and the various effects which each article produced. By turns, the German mentioned the brain, the nerves, the spine, the lungs, the heart, etc.; made sundry investigations, and learned, as well as he could, the condition of each organ, and the state of its functions. The bewildered Delia, hardly knowing her own symptoms, was frequently at a loss for a reply. She endeavored to describe her malady; but so dissimilar, at times, were its developments, that, as she afterward said, she scarcely knew whether she gave a true or a false statement. The examination terminated, Dr. Liston continued for some minutes to write, apparently, in some style of stenography. Having finished his memoranda, he turned to Mrs. Thornton and said,

"I expect, madam, that I shall soon be able to restore your daughter to health. In the course of the day, I shall send her some medicine, with directions for its use; also, a list of regulations which must be scrupulously observed. If any deviation from my rules is allowed, I can not be responsible for the consequences."

The physician's novel mode of procedure, and his authoritative method of speaking, had made so profound an impression upon Mrs. Thornton, that she seemed as taciturn as if she had suddenly taken a vow of perpetual silence. As, however, after two low bows—one to the mother, the other to the daughter—the gentleman was preparing to depart, the lady recovered, in some measure, from the abstraction into which she had been plunged, and asked, "Dr. Liston, what is the matter with my daughter?"

"Absence of sound health," was the Spartan reply of the homeopathist, as he vanished through the doorway, leaving the mother of his fair patient, with her mind in rather an unenviable state of doubt, mistrust, and confusion.

VIII.

IRON.

" Work—for some good—be it ever so slowly!
Cherish some flower, be it ever so lowly!
Labor! all labor is noble and holy:
    Let thy great deeds be thy prayer to thy God."—Mrs. Osgood.

WITH a sigh of inexpressible relief, Charles dismissed his pupils, and remembered that the weekly half-holyday was before him. It appeared like a beautiful oasis in the desert. Although a lover of his profession, his mind had not this day been entirely occupied with his self-enjoined duties. He had been in festival mood, earnestly longing for vacation. During the recess, the boys, in their obtuseness, had stared as they witnessed the confusion of their usually clear-headed teacher, while he indiscriminately marked scores of algebraic signs upon the blackboard, and intermingled with them rude delineations of moss roses, brown cottages, and luxuriant tresses. But the girls, with their keen discernment, and half-developed spirit of romance, whispered, "Mr. Thornton is thinking of his lady." Charles little thought that his pupils were watching his progress in crayon drawing, through the open

window opposite the blackboard. The time for recitation, however, found him active, and wholly devoted to the instruction of the young republicans. But
the hands, pointing to the jubilant hour of dismissal,
had never been so joyfully welcomed. For, in common with all teachers, even the most enthusiastic,
Charles did, now and then, feel the insupportable
ennui attendant upon his labors. He had expatiated
upon the same theorems, till he almost wished that
they had never been demonstrated. He had carried
his pupils to the sources of mighty rivers, till he
began to regret that they had ever been discovered.
He had given class after class descriptions relative
to the ruins of the old world, until the startling idea
was revolving in his mind, whether it would not
have been well for him if the treasures of the
buried cities had never been revealed. Leaving
the school-room, he inhaled with delight the fra-
grant June air, and directed his steps toward the
residence of his noble Adelaide. Before planning
any excursion, he would see her who had promised
to tread life's path by his side, to journey with him
to that Elysium, where joy, labor, and rest are so
harmoniously blended, that neither pain, weariness,
nor alloy of any kind, is combined with the attempts
of the inhabitants for advancement, perfection.

The attention of the Wilmots was so profoundly
absorbed that they did not immediately notice the
entrance of their friend. Adelaide was reading
aloud from "The Vale of Cedars," that thrilling

romance of the lamented Grace Aguilar. Rose had laudably resolved to sew while listening to the narrative, but so deep an interest had been excited, that the work lay neglected in her lap, the needle rusting in her fingers. The eyes of the susceptible girl were suffused with tears, as she heard one sketch after another. The attention of the aged man was concentrated upon his daughter as she read. Adelaide, who always had perfect control over her feelings, gave, with great beauty and effect, the various representations of the author. The trio, in their sympathy for the oppressed Jewess, almost forgot that they were Christians. With quivering lip, Rose asked—

"Are you quite sure, Adelaide, that Jesus was the Messiah?"

Adelaide raised her eyes, and regarded her young sister with a slight frown. Then, closing the book, she said, "If papa has no objection, I will defer the reading till another time."

"Oh, Adelaide," cried the half-frantic girl, "we can not leave Marie in the cells of the Inquisition. We must have the remainder of the story before dinner."

"My dear," began Adelaide, when she was suddenly interrupted by Charles, who now advanced, saying, "I am glad that 'The Vale of Cedars' affords you so much pleasure."

"Oh, Charles," exclaimed Rose, "it is most admirable!"

"What say you, Adelaide?"

"It is assuredly a novel of great power, but it belongs to a class that I should not often read."

"Why?"

"Because of the mental excitement produced. Novels of that description affect the mind as alcoholic stimulants do the body. I prefer those which more resemble life in its present phase. Instead of a series of exciting incidents, I choose the history of mind, and the effect of education and circumstances upon its development."

"Of course, my philosophic friend; what opinion, however, shall we have from this little fluttering Rose?"

"I like those which excite my whole soul. I want one heart-stirring scene after another, till my heart throbs, and my cheek burns."

"And your head aches," interposed Adelaide, with significance. "I do not believe that unnatural excitement is healthful."

"I like both kinds," observed Captain Wilmot; "I can not say which I should select."

"Fortunately," remarked Charles, "we have writers of great excellence in each department. Grace Aguilar herself has contributed to both classes. But, come, Adelaide, may I take you home with me for the remainder of the day? Your father looks so well that we can safely trust him with Rose."

"Yes, indeed," said Rose, proudly, "I am now a

year older than was Adelaide, when she first had the whole care of papa."

"Go, my child," rejoined the father, "if the visit will give you any pleasure. Rose and I will finish 'The Vale of Cedars;' but, no, we will reserve that till you can enjoy it with us, unless," continued he, with a smile, "Rose must have the sequel of the story."

"Oh, do not consider me as a child," entreated Rose; "we will leave 'The Vale of Cedars' till Adelaide can read it with us. This afternoon we can have"—here she repressed a yawn—'Rollin's History.'"

Adelaide could not avoid noticing that, although Charles laughed merrily, there were serious indications of lassitude in his manner.

"You are fatigued," she said, reproachfully; "you have been toiling more than your strength would allow."

"I know it, but I am going to recreate this afternoon. When I entered upon the career of a teacher, I resolved to emulate the ecclesiastic, Henry Arnauld, who, when advised to take one day in the week for recreation, replied, 'I will readily do so, if you will point out any day on which I am not a bishop.' But I find that I can not labor the whole time."

"I revere those Arnaulds," replied Adelaide. "Was not that an admirable answer of Anthony to his opponent, 'Rest! will you not have all eternity to rest in?'"

"You very much resemble those men of iron. I must confess my weakness. I need rest."

"So do we all, my friend. So does every part of our bodies. The heart itself, that indefatigable organ, rests in the intervals of its contractions, actually taking one fourth of the whole time for repose The Arnaulds, doubtless, fulfilled that law of nature which demands rest, otherwise they would not have lived to old age. It is also probable that they refreshed themselves by frequently varying their employments. Will it add to your fatigue to give me a lesson in Greek this afternoon?"

Charles pretended to groan, as he said, "Oh, Adelaide, I have been teaching all the forenoon. I consent, but, being too much exhausted to trust my memory, I shall take the grammar into the woods. There, while the birds are singing, the grass waving, and the leaves fluttering with the zephyr's breath, you shall add to the music by repeating τύπτω, τύπτεις, τύπτει, etc."

"I can not imagine," said Rose, "why my sister is learning Greek. I am content with French and Latin."

"The lore of childhood satisfies the child," quoted Adelaide.

Rose blushed painfully, and made no reply.

"Be not offended, Rosie," expostulated the elder sister; "at your age, I did not think of learning Greek, for the plain reason that it was seldom taught to girls. The same neglect still prevails.

I will educate myself on the plan that I should prescribe for every individual, of either sex, who desires to have a cultivated intellect, and a large share of influence in the world."

"I suspect," remarked Captain Wilmot, "the true reason for Adelaide's Greek studies. She wishes to maintain philological discussions with the minister, in reference to certain obscure passages in the New Testament."

"You misjudge me, my dear father. I am not thinking of controversy. It is, however, my intention to read the New Testament for myself in the original, without depending on any man, or any body of men, for a translation. I must also read, in the language in which they were written, the most valuable classics of antiquity."

"A very good defense," said Charles, "and one which ought to be satisfactory to every person of common intelligence. But, come, I am afraid that we shall be late for dinner. In that case, my mother's welcome will not be very cordial."

"How sorry I am to have you go!" murmured Rose, as she escorted the pair to the door.

"My dear," replied Charles, with mock gravity, 'how can you regret our departure! You will not only have the society of your good papa, but that also of the very instructive Monsieur Rollin."

Rose contorted her pretty features, as she gayly bade him adieu, and replied, that he need not profess to be quite certain respecting the nature of her afternoon's employment.

IX.

HOMEOPATHY.

"Take a little rum,
  The less you take the better;
Mix it with the lakes
  Of Wenner and of Wetter.

"Dip a spoonful out—
  Mind you don't get groggy—
Pour it in the lake
  Winnipisiogee.

"Stir the mixture well,
  Lest it prove inferior;
Then, put half a drop
  Into Lake Superior.

"Every other day,
  Take a drop, in water;
You'll be better soon;
  Or, at least, you ought to.
       $\frac{1}{1,000,000}$."—ANON.

DINNER was served at the mansion of the Thorntons soon after the arrival of our friends. All were eager to hear an account of the visit of the homeopathist. Mrs. Thornton had greatly demurred, when advised to send for him, having no confidence in the ground of his pretensions. She now asserted that it was beyond the power of memory to recall half the circumstances. At least, one hundred questions had been asked. If it were possible, the ho-

meopathist was even more impertinent than Dr.
Perry.

"Impertinent!" exclaimed Mr. Thornton; "Dr.
Perry certainly would plead 'not guilty' to that
charge."

"Oh, no more than physicians, in general, I presume, but I should like to know what lady likes to
be cross-questioned in that manner!"

"Why then send for a physician?" queried
Charles.

"Charles Thornton, do you suppose that we are
going to die for want of medical aid, rather than
wound our delicacy by submitting to the presence
of a physician?"

"No, madam," was her son's grave answer; "the
love of life is too strongly implanted in the human
breast to admit of any result of that description. I
marvel, however, that the ladies do not themselves
become physicians. What say you, Adelaide? I
have always thought that you were intended for the
medical order."

"You are aware, Charles, that several ladies are
already pursuing a course of medical study. Were
I in favorable circumstances, I would most assuredly
join them. I have always perceived an impropri-
ety in the attendance of male practitioners upon
women."

Ella, who had been listening with close attention,
suddenly asked, "Suppose, Adelaide, that you were
actually ill, so that you could not cure yourself,

would you consent to the attendance of a male physician?"

"Certainly, Ella, but I should regard him as a very disagreeable intruder in my sick chamber, and regret the necessity which compelled me to submit to his directions. I should consider the evil as inevitable, reflecting that the barbarous state of society obliged me to tolerate the indelicacy."

When Adelaide harangued, Mrs. Thornton always frowned. To divert his mother's attention from the young lady's wisdom, Charles abruptly asked, "Ella, how should you like to be a lady physician?"

Ella blushed, hesitated, and, finally, answered,

"I hardly know. I think that ladies ought to have physicians of their own sex."

"Charles!" Mrs. Thornton almost screamed, "I do wish that you would not give Ella such ideas. When she leaves school, she will stay at home, like a young lady. To hear you, any one would think that we were too poor to support our daughters."

"Mamma," interposed Ella, very decidedly, "I will do something. If I am not a physician, it will be because the profession does not accord with my taste. But I know that many girls would like very much to investigate subjects connected with the medical art. I do not purpose to lead a life of inglorious ease. I may possibly be the pastor of a church."

The thunderbolt, averted from Adelaide, was now about to fall upon Ella. To turn it aside, Mr. Thornton, after one deprecatory glance at his wife, hastily said, "Come, Delia, tell me something about Dr. Liston's visit."

The young lady smiled. "Well, papa, he asked a great many questions, and recorded the answers as fast as I could give them."

"He must have a very poor memory."

"That does not follow, papa," replied Delia, respectfully; "if his questions to each patient are so numerous, it would be almost impossible for him to remember every answer. He promised to send me some medicine, and a list of regulations, with which I must strictly comply."

"Are you quite willing, Delia, to receive the visits of Dr. Liston? If you object, I will dismiss him."

"I prefer that he should come, papa. His care in tracing every symptom, and his great solicitude to learn the exact truth, could not fail to inspire me with some degree of confidence in his skill."

A ring was now heard at the door bell. After the lapse of some minutes, Dora entered the dining-room, bringing a small package, directed to Miss Thornton. Delia took it, simply saying, "My medicine, I presume."

Dora's eyes were sparkling, and her cheeks glowing with pleasurable excitement.

"I hope, Dora," said Mrs. Thornton, with some asperity, "that you had a pleasant time. Were you looking up street, or down, or what were you doing?"

"Indeed, ma'am," answered the poor girl, with an appearance of great humility, but with a half-suppressed air of triumph, "I stopped only a second?"

"A second! I should like to have you work for me, if your time were composed of seconds of that length. Who brought the medicine?"

"'Twas the gentleman that takes care of the new doctor's horse, and carries round his little powders for him."

Dora now hastily commenced her retreat, without waiting for a rejoinder. The young people, with the sympathy of generous hearts, smiled kindly upon the emigrant girl, but Mrs. Thornton, who now began to anticipate that, at no very distant day, the "gentleman" of whom Dora had spoken, would probably ask her to quit service, and be mistress of a little home of her own, sat the impersonation of rage and disgust.

"Never mind, mamma," said Charles, with a quiet smile, "you have frequently said that Dora was the worst servant whom you had ever employed."

"Mamma," observed Ella, "wishes to retain Dora, for the same reason that prompted the petition of the man, who prayed that the life of his wicked king might be spared."

"What was that?"

"His successor might be still worse."

Mrs. Thornton was about commencing a tirade, upon the interesting topics of audacious children and incompetent domestics, when her eye suddenly fell upon Delia's package, causing her thoughts to flow into quite another channel.

"Open your papers, Delia," she commanded, with so Elizabethan an aspect, that the young lady trembled while she complied.

Unfastening the envelope, she first took out a printed paper, containing the regulations to which the physician had alluded. For a moment, she surveyed it with a look of horror.

"What is it, Delia?" cried the children, in a tone of alarm.

No answer.

"Have mercy, Delia," called Ella, "you look as if Medusa's eyes were before you, instead of that harmless piece of paper."

"I would about as lief be petrified as to obey these rules," replied Delia, who was rather. Apician for a young lady; "I am required to live like a hermit."

"Let us hear some of the rules."

"I must neither eat nor drink any thing of an acid nature. Limes, pickles, currants, and all similar articles are forbidden. I can not even refresh myself with a glass of lemonade during the approaching warm weather."

Charles could not refrain from glancing toward Adelaide, who was tightly compressing her lips, to prevent a smile.

"No lemonade!" exclaimed Ella, with a tragi-comic air, "with all my heart do I commiserate you. Will not cream of tartar, which, in my opinion, is far preferable, be allowed by this rigid homeopathist?"

"I have told you," answered Delia, bitterly, "that no acid is permitted."

"Go, then, to the other extreme. An acid beverage is no more delicious than a saccharine. Take metheglin."

Delia's eye brightened, but, after a moment's pause, assuming an expression of great mystery, she said, "It is very singular that honey is also forbidden. If the acid would injure me, I should certainly think that the saccharine would be beneficial."

"It is not," remarked Adelaide, "that all the articles forbidden would by themselves be detrimental. But, as their properties are medicinal, they would either counteract the homeopathic medicines, or entirely neutralize their effects."

"Ah!" said Delia, quietly, for she was reasonable enough to submit to any rule of which she knew the explanation. But, in the next breath, she groaned, "Coffee and green tea are forbidden. How am I to eat my breakfast?"

"Drink milk and water, as I do," suggested little Carrie.

"I detest milk, as well as cocoa and weak black tea, which, wonderful as it may appear, I have the sanction of the homeopathist for drinking."

"In addition to those, is water the only allowable beverage?" inquired Charles.

"The preference is given to water," answered

Delia, with a slight curl of her lip; "but I perceive that Dr. Liston tolerates several compounds which I know that I could not swallow. Among them are, rice water, plain panada, and sugared water."

"Now, Delia," said Adelaide, playfully, "sugared water was the favorite beverage of the unfortunate Marie Antoinette. If a queen could be satisfied with this simple preparation, surely you might condescend to give it a trial. Why demand any thing more flavorous?"

"I am sure that I should not like so insipid a beverage, if a thousand queens had agreed in its commendation."

"You are then doomed to pure water, the natural drink of man," observed Charles; "if nothing had ever been substituted, from what a catalogue of diseases would the human race have been exempt!"

"Pray, Charles, don't moralize," entreated Delia; "it is highly probable that as early as the innocent days of our first parents, some addition was made to the tasteless beverage provided by nature. When Eve is preparing for Raphael's visit, is water the only liquid procured?

> 'For drink, the grape
> She crushes, inoffensive must, and meaths
> From many a berry, and from sweet kernels press'd
> She tempers dulcet creams.'"

Charles shouted, "My dear sister, if Moses had given that information, I would have conceded to

you the right of pleasing your palate by these foolish substitutes for pure water. But I give no more
credence to Milton's account of the repasts of Eden,
than to his description of the battles between the
good angels and the bad, or to his curious declara-
tions concerning the character of our first mother."

"Charles," denounced Mrs. Thornton, "you are
very irreverent. The Bible speaks of 'the angels
who sinned.'"

"I do not contradict the Bible, mamma, but I
trust my own reason and imagination quite as much
as Milton's. I believe that the Almighty expelled
the sinning angels from heaven, by the immediate
agency of His own power. I will not believe that
He demanded the aid of His loyal subjects, and that
He rendered heaven the scene of fierce contest and
dire confusion. As for Eve, I appeal to all the
young ladies present, whether their conception of
her character corresponds to Milton's."

Delia was silent. Adelaide quoted, "'God is thy
law, thou mine," and commented, "no woman will
respond to that sentiment. Eve knew that Adam
was liable to sin, and that it could not, therefore,
have been safe for her to regard as infallible, any
mandates except those given to them both by the
Creator."

"If," said Ella, eagerly, "Eve's character had
been like that depicted by Milton, she never would
have wished to leave his side, that she might spend
the day in solitude. She would not have said, 'Let

us divide our labors.' She would have preferred to toil with his assistance, and under his protection."

"Really," interrupted Mrs. Thornton, "here is a digression! Strange that people who profess to have well-disciplined minds should wander so far from the subject of conversation!"

"My dear," pleaded Mr. Thornton, who was evidently quite entertained, "do allow the children to proceed. I like to hear them."

"Unless they can say something better than they have yet, I prefer that Delia should go on with those directions."

As the young colloquists were too modest to assert, that they had any thoughts more profound than those to which they had been giving utterance, they signified their wish that Dr. Liston's patient should further enlighten them on the topic of homeopathy.

"I must abstain from pastry," resumed Delia, her eyes resting sadly upon a pyramid of tarts, and the tone of her voice sufficiently indicating the extent of the sacrifice required.

Dora, who was now bringing in the second course, secretly hoped that the whole family would soon be placed under homeopathic treatment.

"Salted fish, ah, that is an article which I never eat."

Nearly all agreed that no self-denial was required in abstaining from this saline delicacy. Mrs. Thornton, however, declared that, in her girlhood, during the palmy days of New England, salted fish was the regular Saturday dinner, and that people were not half so sickly as at the present degenerate period.

Ella audibly rejoiced that "the palmy days of New England" were at an end. Mr. Thornton concurred, saying, "I am truly glad that so absurd a custom has fallen into disuse. I always hated that dinner, and I well remember obviating the necessity of eating much, by securing, in the course of the forenoon, a bountiful luncheon of something more palatable."

"Hard-boiled eggs are condemned. That caps the climax. I would as soon eat an egg in its crude state, as to have it merely plunged into boiling water."

Opinions with regard to eggs were now given; in number, they exactly equaled that of the individuals.

"Would it be possible," inquired Charles, with the solemnity due to so important a question, "for an egg to be boiled quite right?"

"It would not," returned Adelaide, with equal gravity; "even the renowned Vatel must have failed whenever he attempted this most onerous of domestic labors."

"Pork is forbidden."

"You will not, surely, regret that," observed Adelaide, "for it is regarded by all as one of the most indigestible of substances."

"My antipathy to pork," remarked Charles, "is as great as that professed by the Jews, those most inveterate of swine-haters."

After a pause, Delia resumed, with a sigh, "I must eat neither figs nor raisins."

James echoed the sigh, as he took a luscious fig from a tray which had just been brought in with the dessert.

"Spices and condiments of all kinds are forbidden," lamented Delia, in tones which might be called heart-rending.

"But, sister," said Charles, with the air of one soothing a person under the pressure of great affliction, "those can not be of much consequence."

"If you were as well acquainted with cooking as I am," retorted Delia, "you would know that food can not be suitably prepared without condiments."

The large, black eyes of Charles dilated, till they reminded Adelaide of unexplored coal mines. With a low bow, he said to his sister, "I acknowledge that I can not give the exact rule for the filling of a turkey, that I should be at a loss if asked to compound runnet pudding, that I should hesitate if required to superintend the mixing of plum cake, that I should be alarmed if I were solicited even to make a batch of bread, but I do most assuredly believe that I am as well acquainted with the culinary art as yourself."

"Proceed, Delia," said Mrs. Thornton, with an acrid glance at Charles.

"Mineral waters are interdicted."

"That is unfortunate," observed Mr. Thornton; "I have been projecting a trip to Saratoga, believing that the waters would do you more good than the efforts of all the sons of Æsculapius combined."

Delia mused sorrowfully for a moment upon the pleasures of an excursion to the far-famed springs. Then looking at the directions, she said, with a smile, "Ardent spirits and tobacco are prohibited."

"That does not concern you," remarked Charles, laughing.

"I must abstain from eels, clams, oysters, lobsters—"

"I should like to know," ejaculated Mrs. Thornton, "what Dr. Liston will permit you to eat. I can think of nothing."

"There is not much, indeed, mamma. I may eat bread, made without soda, salaratus, etc., plain cake and pudding; squash and potato; beef, mutton, poultry, and venison. Not much more, I believe."

"Very low diet," said Mr. Thornton, shaking his head; "I am afraid that the poor child will lose what little strength she now possesses."

"She will certainly die, without something more nourishing," angrily exclaimed Mrs. Thornton.

"What is better than beef-steak?" pleaded Charles, for, in his own mind, he had been dwelling with admiration upon the beautiful simplicity which

characterized the dietetic code of the homeopathist.

"But, Charles," remonstrated Delia, "homeopathy requires that beef-steak should be cooked without pepper."

"I think, that, even in that case, it might be
quite edible."

Not deigning to reply, Delia continued, "Mutton
is, of course, despicable ; this is not the season for
poultry; venison is seldom brought into Clinton
market."

"Delia, my dear," said Mr. Thornton, in a tone
for which he deserved the surname of Barnabas,
"your mother will, I dare say, carefully study these
directions, and see that as many tempting dishes are
prepared as are possible with so few ingredients.   I
will visit the book-stores, and bring home all the
treatises on cooking that I can find. This is certainly not the season for poultry, but Charles shall
go to Farmer Dean's, and order a regular supply.
I will take care that the greater part of all the venison brought into the neighboring markets shall find
its way to Clinton."

"Delia's eyes were suffused with tears, as she
faintly replied, "You are very kind, papa."

Mrs. Thornton now took the paper, and, holding
it as cautiously as if its contact might impart poison, said, "I never heard of any thing so absurd as
these directions."   After a cursory glance, she said,
"How careless you are, Delia; you omitted one

notice of great importance. You may eat fresh fruit, excepting those kinds which are decidedly acid."

"I like fruit."

All now hastened to congratulate Delia, declaring that fruit was the best food that could be obtained, and asserting that her doom was not half so dismal as they had, at first, imagined.

"I do believe," exclaimed Mrs. Thornton, suddenly, "that Dr. Liston is an idiot!"

This being rather a serious charge to be brought against a medical practitioner, all eagerly raised their eyes, to learn the cause of the accusation.

"All kinds of perfumery are to be avoided. Delia must not even approach odoriferous flowers."

"There, Delia," laughed Ella, "you must remove that bottle of cologne water, from your dressing-table."

James, with unusual alacrity, conveyed from the window-seat, a fine musk plant, and a luxuriant tea-rose bush, which were perfuming the apartment.

After a short discussion, all agreed, that, if condiments would be at variance with Dr. Liston's medicines, odors, in their effects upon the system, might have a certain, although subtile influence, and that, homeopathically speaking, the apparently absurd direction was consistent and reasonable.

"I like that rule," concluded Charles, "as far as concentrated odors are implied. In church, I am sometimes almost faint in consequence of the gale of lavender and bergamot that rushes from Mrs. Stipend's pew into ours."

"Open the other paper, Delia," commanded Mrs. Thornton. Delia carefully unfolded a small paper, containing a diminutive white powder, apparently intended as a moderate dose for an infant Lilliputian. Laying it upon the table with great precaution, lest it should be wafted into the air, she took up a slip of paper, and read, with undisguised amazement: "Miss Thornton may dissolve this powder in a tumbler of water, and take a tablespoonful every morning till it is exhausted."

Not only the children, but also the adults, caused the room to resound with merry laughter. Mr. Thornton had not, for many years, manifested so much risibility. Mrs. Thornton's half-suppressed anger was exchanged for an alarming cachination. Charles had not been so thoroughly amused since the enlivening moment when Alfred Russell, a very ingenious orthographer, wrote *Q* as the initial letter of *curiosity*. Delia's countenance was so animated, that she looked as if she might safely dispense with medicine. Adelaide could not refrain from laughing in sympathy, but, as she was partially acquainted with the homeopathic system, the prescription had occasioned neither mirth nor surprise.

"Homeopathy must be a hoax," said Mr. Thornton, with great emphasis.

"The vile impostor!" exclaimed Mrs. Thornton; "he deserves to be driven from the town."

"Certainly," observed Charles, with an effort at calmness; "this appears like an imposition."

"Papa," said little Carrie, "that doctor would suit me. I hate medicine."

"Still," continued Charles, doubtfully, "we can not yet condemn the system. The remedies administered may be of great power. A very small quantity of arsenic will destroy life. Is it not probable that the homeopathists prepare their medicines so that the quintessence of the ingredients is preserved?"

"I know, I understand how it is, said Mr. Thornton, suddenly erect with unwonted energy. "You remember, my love, the lecture that I attended last winter.

"Really, Mr. Thornton," frigidly replied his wife, "you went to hear lectures six evenings out of seven. You must be a little more explicit if you would have me recall any definite period."

A faint flush passed over the face of the rebuked husband. It soon vanished, and, in deliberate tones, he said, "The lecture was delivered in January, by a young man named Barnard. I forget the subject, but it had some connection with medicine. He said that the founder of homeopathy was a man of the name of—let me see—it began with H; Adelaide, my dear, you know every thing; what was it?"

"It was Hahnemann, sir," answered Adelaide, hardly raising her eyes.

"Oh, yes. Well, this Hahnemann, a very shrewd man, was a firm believer in Mesmerism. But, through fear of the ridicule which would have been his lot, if he had professed his views, he practiced a very unjustifiable system of deception. He mesmerized his medicines, holding the theory that the greater number of times the hand passed over them, the more beneficial would be the effects produced. The smaller the doses, the greater the virtue."

By the aspect of the various members of Mr. Thornton's family, while they had been listening to this explanation, any one would have thought that they had been hearing some of the most direful passages of Scott's " Demonology and Witchcraft." Adelaide remained with her eyes downcast.

Mr. Thornton continued, "The lecturer, at his close, made the audience very merry, by saying that Hahnemann himself would have become a true Democritus, could he have foreseen that glass factories would be established for the express purpose of manufacturing his tiny vials, and that large numbers of respectable physicians would traverse the country, carrying cases of his little powders in their pockets. Whatever mode of practice he professed to follow, Hahnemann was truly of the mesmeric order."

"I wish," regretted Charles, " that I had heard that lecture."

"I advised you to go, my son, but you said that

you could only spare two evenings a week for lectures, and that you had resolved to spend the others in study."

"If I were incapable of reading, I should be a
constant attendant of the lecture-room ; but, having
the power of perusing the printed page, I prefer
that 'eye-gate,' rather than 'ear-gate,' shall be the
chief avenue to my mind. Adelaide, you and I
were reading Marmontel that evening. What do
you think of my father's report ?"

"I doubt the claims of the lecturer to confidence.
Hahnemann probably employed Mesmerism among
other remedial agents. He did believe in the efficacy of medicines, for he was so hazardous as to
try many experiments upon himself. When in
health, he took medicinal substances as an adven-
turer, to learn their effects upon the system. He
convinced himself that the true remedy for any disease would produce the same malady in a healthy
person. This was his own view. I am not competent to decide upon its merits. The reason which I
have learned for the small doses, has some shade of
plausibility. The chemist and the advanced medical student must weigh its validity. Homeopathists believe that medicinal properties are lost by
combination. They maintain that, for the advantage of friction, or some other effect, the drug used
should be subjected to repeated divisions, that it
may be given in, as nearly as possible, an atomic
state."

The Thorntons, without speaking, looked alternately at each other and at Adelaide.

After conveying the condemned plants from the dining-room to the garden, James, who had not been very deeply interested in the discussion of homeopathy, strolled leisurely through the grounds in quest of amusement. Passing into the street, he espied a loose paper fluttering upon the door-step. Supposing it to be one of the numerous hand-bills which are now scattered in such profusion over the land, he proceeded to investigate its contents, laudably desirous of learning whether it announced the virtues of a patented medicament, the programme of a marvelous exhibition, or the prospectus of a new book. He soon perceived that it was covered with characters, which, to him, were as inscrutable as the Eleusinian mysteries to the uninitiated. So attractive, however, were the curiously arranged dots, straight lines, and curves, that he carried the paper into the house, earnestly soliciting an explanation.

"Why, Jamie," said Charles, "this must be a specimen of some system of stenography. But it is not Holdsworth's, and I am unacquainted with any other."

"It is phonography," asserted Adelaide, "the best system ever invented. The adept can write as rapidly as the speaker can pronounce."

"That writing, then," observed Mr. Thornton, "may contain notes of a sermon or lecture."

" Or it may be a theme," suggested Ella.

" Whatever it is," said Charles, with more decision than was needed, "I presume that we have
a right to avail ourselves of its wisdom, especially
as we are so fortunate as to have an interpreter.
Had it been a secret paper, the owner would have
been more prudent than to carry it through the
street in his pocket.   As no name is attached, it is,
for the present, the property of the finder.   By
reading it, we can learn whether it is of consequence
to the possessor.   If it is a paper of importance, we
can insert an advertisement in the ' Chronicle.' "

" You must have conscientious scruples with respect to the perusal, or you would not give so elab-
orate a defense," remarked his father, with a half
smile.

Charles laughingly replied, "I firmly believe
that it is my duty to learn the contents of that
paper.   I by no means consider it a question of
casuistry."

All inspected the paper before Adelaide began
the translation.

" It may be a conspiracy against the government," said Mr. Thornton.

" Equal to that of Catiline," subjoined Adelaide.

" It has a very wicked look," said Mrs. Thornton,
almost dropping the paper from her hands.

" Allay your fears," said Adelaide, gayly, as she
glanced at the paper; "I see nothing of dangerous
import.   It is apparently a sketch of character,

intended for full delineation at the writer's leisure. No title is given.

" Size of the head, full. Temperament, a combination of the nervous and the lymphatic. The latter predominant. The former developed by circumstances. Much revealed by the organs of the head, more than by her answers. Perceptive faculties better developed than the reflective. Appearance of the head singular, from the unusual prominence of some organs, and the defective size of others. *Combativeness* wanting, hardly force enough to resist either disease or danger. *Alimentiveness* excessive for a young lady. *Firmness*, minus. *Hope*, ditto. *Individuality*, very prominent. *Form*, so prominent that the distance between the eyes is quite startling. A striking, but not a good head. Figure, too slender for health or beauty. No definite disease, but a general want of tone to the system. Pulse, weak; complexion, inclining to sallow; manner of speaking, languid; expression of countenance, listless.

Needs some incitement to mental and bodily action, rather than any course of medicine. So feeble, however, has the frame been rendered by bad habits, that some medicine is needed. Tendency to incipient disease must also be counteracted by the application of remedies. Tedious case in perspective. Delia Thornton, nineteen years, three months."

The Thorntons had listened with close attention. Notes of a phrenological lecture—abstract of a medical student's lesson—were among the first impressions. But, as the reading approached its termination, they suddenly started, exchanged glances one with another, and when Adelaide, after a momentary hesitation, read Delia's name and age, no one was surprised.

"The impudent man!" exclaimed Mrs. Thornton.

"Was that what Dr. Liston was writing?" asked Mr. Thornton.

"That must have been one of the papers," sobbed Delia. "He apparently made two accounts. After recording the answers which I gave him, he wrote in silence for some minutes. I noticed that the leaf was detached. It must have dropped from the book."

"Is Phrenology connected with homeopathy?" inquired Charles.

"No," replied Adelaide; "but, being acquainted with Phrenology, Dr. Liston wisely applies it to his profession. By learning the mental organization of his patients, he can form a very good estimate of the class of diseases to which they are most liable."

"Delia," cried Ella, "do remove your handkerchief from your face, that we may see whether your eyes are really so far apart."

"A striking, but not a good head," cited Mr. Thornton, with anxiety.

"Figure too slender for health or beauty," repeated Mrs. Thornton, in wrathful accents. "If Dr. Liston were not a dunce, he would know that a slender figure is considered beautiful."

"That idea is now exploded, madam," answered Charles.

"The Venus de Medicis is represented with a large waist," observed Adelaide.

"Tedious case in perspective," muttered Mr. Thornton.

Meanwhile Delia's appearance was indicative of extreme distress. Her affliction probably resembled that of English girls when excluded from Almack's.

"Delia," expostulated her father, "that whole account is contemptible. I would not give it a moment's thought."

"Besides, Delia," added Charles, "people differ in their taste. Some would call you beautiful, especially if your countenance were irradiated by health and vivacity."

"I will not have him for my physician," declared Delia.

Charles smiled as he said, "Dr. Liston did not read your head aright. If you were devoid of combativeness, you would have neither the courage nor the desire to refuse his attendance. You would bear his strictures with meekness."

"I will never again see him," persisted Delia.

"Delia has some firmness," remarked Ella.

"If she had much," returned Charles, "she would abide by her first decision, and retain Dr. Liston, notwithstanding this little incident."

"Little!" repeated Delia, in a tone which reminded Adelaide of Hermia's utterance of the same word.

"What is your opinion, Adelaide?" asked Charles.

"If all the physicians and phrenologists in the world had pronounced a verdict which I knew to be false, my equanimity would not be seriously disturbed."

Delia was silent. Perhaps she knew that Dr. Liston's description contained more truth than error.

"The man shall never again enter my house," said Mrs. Thornton, with dignity.

"We can not, then, test the value of homeo-pathy," observed Mr. Thornton.

"This would hardly deserve the name of a test," replied Charles. "Dr. Liston himself acknowledges that Delia is not actually ill. I regret, however, that we found the paper. The observance of those dietetic directions would probably have cured Delia. Would it not be well to overlook the circumstance of the note-taking, and allow him to make a series of visits? It will be hardly courteous to dismiss him because we found and read a paper containing his private opinion."

"Yes, Delia," said Ella, "those directions may be very beneficial. In Dr. Liston's view, your illness has been caused partly by too assiduous a cultivation of the organ of alimentiveness."

"Silence, Ella!" angrily demanded her mother.

"I have decided," repeated Delia, in a manner implying that it was her purpose to acquire a reputation for firmness.

"Well," said Charles, resignedly, "you would doubtless soon violate those strict rules, and then Dr. Liston would voluntarily discontinue his visits. I heard yesterday that he had been attending Henry Richardson, a young man of twenty-three, for some serious malady. After weeks of great pain, convalescence slowly but surely began. The hungry patient entreated that the regulations might be slightly modified. The physician was inexorable, declaring that no deviation could be allowed. On his next visit, after looking at Henry a few minutes, he said, 'Sir, you have disobeyed me. What have you been eating?' The poor young man stammered through an apology, confessing, that being unable to relish any of the articles permitted, he had eaten sparingly of veal cutlets, and that he really felt better for the indulgence. Without a word, the homeopathist left the room, encountered the senior Richardson upon the stairs, and quietly announced that he must procure another physician for his son."

"Dr. Liston shall not rule me," exclaimed Delia, with unusual energy.

"Physicians, by their profession," observed Adelaide, "have the right to command. We voluntarily surrender ourselves as their subjects. We can not, therefore, complain if they demand implicit obedience."

"Yes," said Ella, eagerly, "'*must* is for the doctor as well as for the king;' so Miss Sedgwick's Mary Bond told her brother."

After a pause, Mr. Thornton said, "We have, then, the disagreeable task of dismissing Dr. Liston," and he looked at Delia to see whether any sign of relenting appeared.

"Remember, Delia," cautioned Charles, "that he is the only physician in the place, besides Dr. Perry."

"I have decided," replied Delia, with the firmness of a martyr preferring "the baptism of fire" to a renunciation of his faith.

Mr. Thornton bit his lip, and mused in silence. After a few moments of disquiet, he said, "Charles, I think that either you or your mother would do better than myself."

Charles, shrinking from the office on his own account, and deeming it unadvisable that his mother should address the physician in her salamandrine style, replied. "In my opinion, sir, as Delia has a father, it would be more proper that the rejection should be given by him."

"You are right, my son," said Mr. Thornton, suddenly recollecting that he was the head of the family, "but I dread the interview."

"Write to him, sir," suggested Charles.

Half an hour afterward, as Dr. Liston was sitting in his study, preparing minimum doses of aconite, he received a note, inclosing the paper which he had lost, and containing the following words: "Dr. Liston is informed that the knowledge of phonography is not confined to himself, that it is very dangerous to have loose leaves in a private note-book, and that he need give himself no further trouble with regard to the 'tedious case' of Miss Thornton."

X.

M. D. AND D. D.

"A waking eye, a prying mind,
A heart that stirs, is hard to bind,
A hawk's keen sight ye can not blind."—C. LAMB.

LATE one Saturday afternoon, the Rev. Dr. Leland seated himself in his study to compose a sermon for the ensuing Sabbath. He was not one of
those provident preachers who have, in advance,
twenty elaborately-written discourses. He had frequently deprecated the necessity of penning so
many pages every week. In hating task-work, he
resembled the mighty "Magician of the North."
But he consoled himself with the thought that both
the animate and the inanimate creation are subject
to laws, that even the superb planets have their
regular orbits to describe. In his preparation for
the pulpit, he was too apt to depend upon the inspiration of the moment. If the educated portion
of his audience sometimes observed that thought
and study were better than mere human inspiration,
he might have replied, that if he did occasionally
give them only a rhapsody, they must cheerfully

submit to their fate, as he did to his, when compelled to visit scores of people, with whom he had no sympathy, save that of the pastoral relation.

Like the venerable White, "he was born for a bishop." A dissenting bishop, however, for his parents, being strict Congregationalists, had impressed upon the infant mind of their son so great a horror of the surplice and prayer-book, that he could never have been deemed sufficiently unprejudiced to examine the claims of the Church of England. Had he been educated as an Episcopalian, he would, after taking holy orders, have persevered till he had reached the highest point of church preferment. In his own class, he was not content till he had received the honor of Doctor of Divinity.

He was destined to rule in some way. As the chances of birth had made him a citizen of republican America, of that part, too, which was inhabited by the descendants of the Pilgrims, he gave a willing ear to the admonitions of his father and mother, when they told him that no man was greater than he who bore the title of Rev. His early years were passed in anticipations of the sacred office. Born in a country town, he saw that his own pastor was the greatest man in the place. He learned, also, that the clergy of New England had always been regarded with veneration approaching to awe. With a full share of the imitative powers of childhood, his every juvenile amusement was a fac-simile of some clerical performance of the Rev. Mr. Hol-

den.   His ignorant parents regarded him as a
prodigy of infantine piety.   His extemporaneous
sermons to his brothers and sisters, the length and
fervor of his morning and evening devotions, were
duly proclaimed to all the gossiping friends of the
farmer and his wife.   Meantime, the heart of the
child was no more renewed than that of his little
neighbor, who sedulously mimicked the rural tasks
of the ploughman.

As the scene of his nativity afforded no facilities
for the acquirement of a liberal education, young
Leland was fortunately sent from home to a place
where more enlarged ideas were the inseparable at-
tendants of knowledge and refinement.   His character now underwent many important changes.   In
the course of his preparatory studies, he learned,
that, in a worldly point of view, the clerical was
far from being the highest of distinctions.   Ambition, he possessed by nature, and it had been fearfully fostered by his simple-minded parents.   Great,
he would be, in some vocation.   The records of the
historic scroll were consulted with avidity.   The
highest offices in the country were surveyed with an
eager eye.   The recipient of legal honors, the head
of the proudest university in the land, the mightiest
general of the army, even the occupant of the pres-
idential chair, were seriously pondered and discussed by the young scholar.   In his own opinion,
he had talents that would qualify him for any station that he might select.   His humble parents, far

away in the country, read his letters with deep anxiety, and expressed to each other their fears that he
would never be a minister.

The ambitious youth had nearly finished his collegiate career. He was daily considering the question of his future path, when, an apparently trivial
incident caused his heart to beat in unison with
that of his parents, and his wish to echo to that
which he had formed, when, as a little child, he
clasped his hands, and prayed that he might hereafter stand in the pulpit, and speak to the people.

The last term of the senior year was drawing to
its close. A beautiful Sabbath morning had dawned. The class, that was so soon to graduate, slowly
entered the chapel to listen to the President's sermon. Leland was not the only irresolute student.
Others there were, who had nearly completed the
collegiate course, without deciding upon the studies
that should succeed. As the President looked
around, his thoughts dwelt with peculiar solicitude
upon those who were so soon to be removed from
his influence. His love for the church was as fer-
vid as that felt by the parents of one, at least, of
his pupils. It exceeded theirs in intelligence, in
proportion to the greater depth and extent of his
attainments. In their mental and social insignificance, they revered the clergyman for his position;
from his elevated point of view, he honored him
for his noble sphere of usefulness, and for his large
allotment in the regeneration of mankind.

Far away from that quiet room were the thoughts of young Leland, as, with his face mechanically turned toward the preacher, he patiently awaited the utterance of the text. In mild, earnest tones, melodious from deep feeling, the President pronounced the words:

"How beautiful upon the mountains are the feet of him that bringeth good tidings, that publisheth peace; that bringeth good tidings of good, that publisheth salvation; that saith unto Zion, Thy God reigneth!"

Then followed a forcible delineation of the true grandeur of the office held by the Christian minister. Nor was the picture one of unbroken light. Reproach and penury were enumerated among the possible trials of the herald of salvation. On the other hand, the elevated nature of the office was exhibited, the consciousness which the faithful man of God must always possess of his extensive co-operation with the King of the whole earth, the Sovereign of the vast universe. Brief but thrilling sketches were given of the gentle Oberlin, with his Christ-like benevolence; of the eloquent Hall, with his vivid, effective style; of the zealous Wickliffe, with his stern resistance to all that he deemed error.

Leland left the chapel, his heart agitated by new emotions. The sermon had been the turning-point in his career. He no longer wavered in his decision. But another question now arose. The Pres-

ident had warmly maintained that no worldly heart
should be offered for the especial work of the Lord,
that no mind unpurified from the pollution of sinful
thought and unholy passion, could hope for accept-
ance as a bearer of the gospel standard. Leland
struggled in agony, at the remembrance of his
Pharisaical childhood, of his selfish, scheming
youth; but, before the sun of that memorable Sabbath had ceased to illumine his path, he had solemnly renounced the sins of his previous life, the
cravings of his restless heart for the distinctions
conferred by man, and had humbly pledged himself
to the service of the Supreme. He was truly honest.
He sincerely intended to follow the true and the
right, but his ambition, although modified, still remained. No prouder heart beat than that which
throbbed in his bosom even after long years of
effort at self-conquest. Although purified from sin,
the soul still retains the impression of the evil
which marred its original beauty.

He had accepted the pastoral care of the first
church of Clinton, a town far exceeding his native
place in size and power, but a mere village in comparison with the great cities of the land. During
the early part of his ministry, he had hoped soon to
"receive a call" to a wider sphere of action. Years,
however, passed away, and, although the aspiring
clergyman was known as a faithful pastor, a thorough scholar, and a good pulpit orator, no church
ever asked him to leave his little flock in the wil-

derness. By degrees, he ceased to wish for a change. He became attached both to the place and the people. There was another and more cogent reason yet unacknowledged perhaps by himself. The importance of his office in that comparatively small town, and his authoritative, although courteous and agreeable manner, had given him so great an ascendency, that he might be said to bear absolute sway in all matters both of church and state.

Such was the character of the man who, having, within a few minutes, finished his morning sermon, was now rapidly writing one destined for the afternoon. With a pen, the fleetness of which would have terrified the deliberate Foster, he was hurrying over the surface both of his paper and his subject, noting texts, arguments, and illustrations with telegraphic speed, when a loud ring at his doorbell caused him to groan in a manner which betokened that the spirit of resignation was not at that moment triumphant. He could not forbear glancing from the window, with the hope that the caller might be a friend of his wife, or if, indeed, parish business demanded his attention, she might act as his substitute. He almost tottered back into his chair, exclaiming, "Dr. Perry! of all the bores in Christendom, he is the last person whom I wish to see!"

By this time, the intrusive guest was rapidly advancing over the stairs. In one moment a brisk knocking was heard upon the study door. The clergyman arose, pen in hand, and, with an expression of countenance which plainly indicated, "I can spare you only a few minutes," welcomed his visitor.

Dr. Perry scanned the perplexed visage of his host with a curious, slightly malicious, and perfectly comprehensive eye. Then, quietly seating himself, and bestowing upon the inchoate sermon a look of dire indignation, he said, with the comfortable air of a man who has hours at his disposal, "I hope, Dr. Leland, that we are not to be favored with a Saturday afternoon sermon."

"It is doubtful," replied his pastor, with equal composure; "you may have a Saturday night sermon."

"In that case, you will not complain, if as many of your parishoners as are aware of the fact, attend some other place of worship on the morrow."

Now, if any subject of minor importance was a source of annoyance to Dr. Leland, it was the occasional practice of some of his people, of resorting to the newly-established churches of Clinton. Could he have had his own will, they would never have heard any preacher but himself, or those of his clerical brethren whom he deigned to select. He therefore answered in a tone of pique, "Strange that those who own pews in one church, should be willing to go to another every few Sabbaths, and to be dependent upon charity for seats."

"Courtesy, not charity, my dear sir. It is outrageous, however, that you should give us sermons written when you are fatigued by the labors of the week."

"You know very well," replied Dr. Leland, struggling to repress his rage, "that this is not my usual mode."

"The variations, then, are alarmingly frequent. Do you not remember the couplet,

> "'Oft turn your style, if you would write
> Things that will bear a second reading.'

Rather than hear two poor sermons, your people would readily consent to the repetition of a good one."

"I may give them their choice some day," replied the clergyman, with a look of combined fierceness and dignity.

Dr. Perry, who had come for the express purpose of asking a favor, began to think it not very politic to preface his request by any further display of his sincerity. Changing his tone, he entertained his pastor with ludicrous stories of certain refractory patients whom he had been attending, till both the sermon and the interruption were floating far away over the waters of Lethe. When he had carefully opened a way for his petition, he said, "Dr. Leland, I want you to preach a sermon on the evils of homeopathy, and some other foolish systems of medical practice."

The risible muscles of Dr. Leland's face were, for

a moment, subjected to strict discipline. At length, he said, sportively, " You would deprive me of the preacher's chief advantage, the choice of his subject."

"Is that your opinion? I always thought it as difficult to select a subject as to write a theme. Besides, does not Campbell say that one great advantage of the lawyer and the senator over the preacher is, that as the subject is announced, the people have their curiosity excited, and their minds in an intelligent state to accompany the discourse. I believe that if you were to notify your people every Sabbath of the subjects of your next two sermons, the hearers would not only be more numerous, but also better prepared to profit by your efforts. The church was thronged on the day which you had appointed for your Californian sermon. I never witnessed a more attentive audience."

"But you forget, Dr. Perry, that, with a money-loving population, a speaker could hardly urge a more powerful incentive, than a discourse relating to the all-absorbing gold of California. Besides, no very startling appeal to the conscience was expected on that occasion. Suppose that, at the close of the services to-morrow afternoon, I were to say, 'The subject of scandal will be discussed on the next Lord's day.' Should I have a large audience? In my opinion a good proportion would be absent, that they might not virtually acknowledge their need of admonition upon that topic."

"Now, Dr. Leland, is that the result of your study of human nature? Not one man or woman in Clinton would suspect his or her personal guilt. All would come to hear their neighbors lectured."

Dr. Leland smiled as he answered, "While I differ from you, I must continue to officiate in my own way. The people, being ignorant of my intentions, come to church according to custom. By the laws of good breeding, they are compelled to remain, and hear whatever I choose to say to them. I well remember the difficulty with which I preserved my gravity one Sabbath, not many years from the date of my first settlement in Clinton. In politics, I chanced to differ from the majority. I need not tell you that nearly all the people now vote for the candidate whom I prefer—"

Dr. Leland's auditor must certainly have thought that some object of great interest was becoming discernible from the clergyman's window; for, contrary to all the laws of etiquette, he rose from his chair, and stood where he could look directly into the main street. He presently returned, and, with a singularly demure expression of countenance, requested a continuation of the narrative.

"In the course of a certain sermon, I spoke in condemnatory strains of a distinguished man who had lately died. The members of the party to which he had belonged hardly retained their places. It was torture to them to hear any dispraise of their departed hero. One violent politician left the house, but, to my great amusement, all the others remained.. Had I announced my intention, how many, think you, would have been present ?"

" Quite as many, I presume. They would have come from motives of curiosity. But," here the physician paused a moment, "you are a coura- geous man, Dr. Leland. Some clergymen would never dare to introduce a subject hostile to the feelings of the majority."

All the fire in Dr. Leland's nature was roused. From his appearance, one would have thought that a disastrous mental ignition was about to ensue.

" As an ambassador of the Lord," he replied, " I shall always tell my people the truth, without re- gard to consequences. As they voluntarily ap- pointed me for their spiritual guide, they are bound to hear the message of Jehovah as I choose to give it to them. They may dismiss me if they like. I have no objection."

" We much prefer that you should remain," de- clared the physician, acting as spokesman for the whole First Church of Clinton ; " but, did the poli- tician to whom you referred ever allude to your condemnation of the man whom he would have deified ?"

" Never," returned Dr. Leland, with a triumphant smile. " The only rebuke which I received was from Charles Thornton, who was then a mere boy. The thought of it has frequently rendered me quite merry. He called the next day, and, after apologizing for the freedom he was about to employ, began, 'Dr. Leland, do you think it quite right to speak evil of the dead? Should they not be allowed to slumber peacefully in their graves?'

"Had my reprover been a man, I should have driven him from my presence, and then have spent the next week in remorse for my precipitancy. But the youth, frankness, modesty, and simplicity of this second Elihu, caused me to hear him without anger. I made him sit down, and then said, 'Now, Charlie, I like your forbearance with respect to the sins and errors of those whose judgment is with God. But we must look at a subject from more than one point of view. To delude people with the idea that a distinguished man, of unquestionably immoral character, is dwelling in the regions of the blessed, instead of suffering the retribution due to his crimes, is as great an injury to the cause of religion as can well be inflicted. It is apparently very hard to speak of one who has gone from us as devoid of a good title to heaven; but, it is far worse to eulogize every departed person, whatever his merits. Incomparably better was the Egyptian custom of subjecting the dead to a public trial, to ascertain whether they were indeed worthy of the rite of sepulture.'"

The mention of the name of Thornton had recalled the physician's wandering thoughts to the purpose of his visit.

"There, Dr. Leland," he abruptly exclaimed,

without noticing the anecdote, "what do you think of those Thorntons?"

"Think," said the clergyman slowly, as if in doubt as to the design of the question, "why, that they are a very fine family. I number them among my warmest friends."

The physician's large, bushy eyebrows were drawn over his cavernous orbs of vision, rendering his aspect very perceptibly terrific. Dr. Leland slightly shuddered, but said nothing to elicit any communication. At length, Dr. Perry ejaculated, in a mastiff style of utterance, "I hope that you do not consider that termagant a very fine woman."

"To whom do you refer?" inquired the clergyman, with dignity.

"To Mrs. Thornton, of course, that infernal woman, in whose person I believe that the three furies are combined."

"Dr. Perry, if you would not have me instantly compose my sermon on Scandal, and preach it to you this very afternoon, you must modify your censures in some degree."

"But, Dr. Leland, can you endure that woman?"

The clergyman paused a moment, and then slowly replied, "She is assuredly a woman of high temper, which is, I fear, not always under control, but I can not believe that you are justified in speaking as you have within these few minutes."

Dr. Perry riveted upon the figures of the carpet an expressive scowl. He presently observed, in suppressed tones, "You are not fully qualified to judge of Mrs. Thornton. People array themselves in their best appearance when they expect to see their clergyman."

Dr. Leland amused himself a few seconds with wondering whether Dr. Perry had donned his "best appearance" that afternoon. He then asked,

"But what is the matter? Has any thing especially disagreeable occurred between you and Mrs. Thornton?"

Here was an alluring question. The physician grasped it with joy. He now had a fine opportunity for revealing all his recent troubles. He gave a detailed account of Mrs. Thornton's deportment at various times, ending with a pathetic description of the insult offered to a learned practitioner by the burning of his recipe.

"But, what can I do for you?" asked the clergyman, after listening with exemplary patience. "If the lady had confessed her errors to me, I would have given the best advice in my power, almost regretting that I was not a priest of the Church of Rome, that I might impose some weighty penance, to render her more cautious with regard to her besetting sin. Why have you told me all this?"

"The fact is, Dr. Leland, seven of my best families are now believers in homeopathy."

The clergyman could not conquer his inclination to laugh. In his efforts he coughed so convulsively, that the physician began to exercise his professional prerogative, by loosening his cravat, and inflicting several quick, sharp blows upon the cervical vertebræ. This summary process soon relieved the victim, who, struggling to free himself from the hands of the physician, gasped, " I wonder whether one of Dr. Liston's little white powders would not have been as efficacious as that barbarous mode of treatment."

The two gentlemen laughed in concert, the clergyman removing the perspiration from his face with a handkerchief, and the physician still inspecting him with an appearance of great anxiety. Dr. Leland finally drew a long breath, and pronounced himself in a state of convalescence, but he obstinately refused to tell why he had exhibited such obvious symptoms of suffocation. He merely observed, that, owing to some constitutional peculiarity, he had frequently suffered in the same way when eating or laughing.

" Your eating and laughing, then, should be performed with great moderation," said the physician, ominously shaking his head.

Dr. Leland bowed, as if he would observe due compliance with these important directions. Still the restless physician was unsatisfied. Throwing open a blind, he placed a chair in an advantageous position, drew a strip of ivory from his pocket, and, with the dogmatic air of his class, said, " Your case ought to receive immediate attention. Take this chair, and throw back your head. I will press your

tongue with this ivory, that I may have a good view
of your throat.   The larynx may be obstructed, the
epiglottis may be—"

"Excuse me, doctor, I am in perfect health," replied the clergyman, with a smile, as he established
himself in a remote part of the room.

Dr. Perry was hardly willing to believe this statement, so inspiriting had been the hope of a future
surgical operation upon the throat of his revered
pastor.   Being disappointed of even the examination, he resumed, "I think, sir, that you ought to
preach on the subject which I mentioned.   The
homeopathists are deceiving the public."

Dr. Leland sighed.   The expression of his countenance was, for a moment, that of utter helpless-
ness.   Then, hoping to prevent a repetition of the
request, he said, "This will not last long, dear sir.
The Thorntons have already dismissed Dr. Liston."

"Ah, how did it happen?   Who told you?"

"Yesterday, James and Ella were visiting my
children.   I am always amused with Ella's conversation.   She is a true original.   Feeling low-spirited,
I called her into my study.   The effect upon my
weary brain was as enlivening as David's music
upon the harrowed heart of Israel's first monarch.
She chatted about her studies, her great plans for
the future, and her embryo ideas upon theology.   I
could not avoid the conviction that no common destiny was in store for the child.   She ended with a
playful account of Delia's illness, and the discharge

of her two physicians. It appears that Dr. Liston had written, in phonography, a description of his patient. He very carelessly lost the paper. James, the finder, was quite bewildered by its aspect. Adelaide Wilmot was that day dining with the Thorntons. Her knowledge is as versatile as could be desired. Unfortunately for the homeopathist, phonography is numbered among her acquirements. She deciphered the mystic characters. The consequences were, violent weeping and sobbing from Delia, and the dismissal of her physician."

Dr. Perry gleefully rubbed his hands.

"All honor to the fair Adelaide. She was never a favorite of mine, but she shall be from this moment."

"Why have you disliked the young lady?"

"The word *dislike* does not accurately express the sentiment which I have entertained for her. *Exasperation* would be more explicit. I have sometimes been almost enraged during my visits at Captain Wilmot's, by the number and variety of Adelaide's questions. I will give you a specimen: 'Dr. Perry, will you tell me what connection there is between my father's disorder, and the remedy which you have prescribed? Dr. Perry, what is your opinion concerning the air of a crowded room? Is its impurity occasioned chiefly by the cutaneous or by the pulmonary exhalations of the occupants? Dr. Perry, I have learned that the waters of Saratoga are cathartic. Why then should you have sent

Mrs. Allen to that place? The medicine which you previously gave her was of a different order.' I thought that I should be distracted. I finally told her that I was not in the habit of taking medical students, and even if I were, I would not admit her to my classes, for she would first rival and then surpass me, as Abelard did his master, the great philosopher, William des Champeaux."

" I presume that the impudence of your remarks was counterbalanced by the implied compliment."

" Oh, Adelaide's temper is perfect. She is too intent upon the acquisition of knowledge to quarrel with any one. The other day, I heard her conversing with a farmer about the rotation of crops."

"Poor man! I wonder which party communicated information. Some time since, she was in the habit of harassing me with questions in theology. They were more puzzling than any which I had pondered in the Divinity School."

" Why," interrupted the physician, " Adelaide is one of our church members. Is she heretical? Her opinions ought certainly to be confirmed by this time."

" Be not alarmed, my good sir. In all essential points, Adelaide is a firm believer. But she likes to contemplate curious and difficult problems, to talk

> "'Of providence, foreknowledge, will, and fate;
> Fix'd fate, free will, foreknowledge absolute.'"

"Then you have been examined in theology, and

I in pathology, by this most active-minded of querists. Yet, in general society, no one would deem her inquisitive."

"For the plain reason, that she is more thoroughly educated, or rather self-educated, than the majority even of intelligent people. But introduce a stranger, who is acquainted with any subject of general interest that is unfamiliar to her mind, and see whether his power as a teacher is not tested."

"But, does she still cross-question you in theology?"

"Oh, no. I finally lost patience, and said to her, 'Adelaide, men spend years in the study of the Scriptures in the original. How can you expect to cope with them? You should receive their explanations with deference.' She paused a moment, and then, with a very comic look, replied, 'I have already begun to learn Greek. When I can read that with fluency, I shall commence Hebrew. I can then translate for myself.' Thus ended our last conversation upon theology."

The clergyman and his guest, in discussing the character of Adelaide, had quite forgotten the lateness of the hour. Both started with surprise, when the rays of the setting sun flashed through the Venetian blinds of the western window. Dr. Leland cast a glance of dismay upon his unfinished sermon. Dr. Perry rose in haste, saying, "Remember my request."

"Oh, my dear sir, I am totally ignorant of the

subject, and therefore incompetent for such an attempt. Besides, where should I find an appropriate text?"

"I will call some day next week, and give you the benefit of my assistance. We can make a very good sermon. I will give some general medical statements. You shall intersperse them with religious observations. Afterward, we can look through the concordance for a text."

Dr. Leland absolutely refused to aid in the fabrication of a patch-work sermon. Dr. Perry, in his eager remonstrances, gave so little heed to the direction of his hands, that a violent impulse was imparted to a bottle of ink, which was standing in fatal proximity to the literary labors of his pastor. The two sermons, the finished and the unfinished, were completely saturated with the ebon liquid. A scream of horror burst from their author.

"Dr. Perry, you ought to be condemned to preach to-morrow in my stead."

"My dear sir, you do not bear the accident with the heroism of Sir Isaac Newton, when papers far more valuable than these were casually destroyed."

"No, I feel more like Ariosto than Newton."

"I doubt whether you ever felt like Ariosto in your life. To what occasion can you refer?"

"To the day when, having heard a potter repeat some of his verses with a bad accent, he rushed into the shop of the offending artisan, and destroyed a great number of the utensils which he had been manufacturing. In answer to the complaints of the mechanic, the angry poet said, 'I have not sufficiently revenged myself on thee; I have broken only a few pots, and thou hast spoiled the most beautiful of compositions to my face.'"

"Oh, Dr. Leland, what a comparison! Your modesty deserves commendation. I beg that you will come to my office, and burn some of my recipes, or break a good number of my vials. However, I do sincerely regret my carelessness. Have you nothing else prepared?"

"Not a single page."

"Did not Sir Walter Scott write two sermons in a night?"

"Yes; but the novelist was not obliged to preach the next day. He wrote them for a young friend, who, to his credit, was too conscientious to avail himself of the intended kindness."

"I will be content with two extemporaneous sermons."

"You are not the sole representative of my church."

"Is it too late to procure an exchange?"

"Certainly. I would not ask one of my brethren at this late hour of the week."

Dr. Perry was, in reality, more troubled than he chose to express. He walked to a window, and listlessly gazed upon the landscape. Suddenly, he exclaimed, "Joy, joy, my friend! Look down this **road.** I see very plainly a chaise, containing two of your clerical friends, Messrs. Hildreth and Sutherland. They are doubtless coming to make you a visit. Each of them probably has a sermon in his pocket."

The two friends, for such they were, despite their eccentricities, joined in a rapturous embrace. Dr. Leland laughingly observed, "I have sometimes heard you complain both of the discourses and the delivery of those gentlemen."

"No matter, I will go to church both parts of the day, as a penance for ruining your sermons. I may possibly rise at the close of the afternoon service, and offer an additional prayer, a very fine one that I saw in a newspaper the other day; 'Oh, Lord, forgive the tediousness of the speakers, and the weariness of the hearers. Amen.' Now, I will leave you to receive the orators of the ensuing Sabbath."

XI.

HYDROPATHY.

"J'ai commencé anjourd hui la douche; c'est une assez bonne répétition du purgatoire."—MME. DE SÉVIGNÉ.

FOR some days, the senior members of the Thornton family were undecided in their plans. Delia was far from well. They could not call upon either of the resident physicians, and they shrank from the idea of sending to the metropolis for medical aid. That would indeed appear as if she were dangerously ill. They seriously thought of going to Saratoga, without knowing whether or not the waters would agree with her constitution. A new idea was soon suggested. The advertisement of the hydropathist had received but little attention. Now, however, that a Clintonian, Mr. Robert Elbridge, had returned from a Water-Cure establishment, with renewed health and vigor, they began to think more frequently of the claims of Priessnitz and his disciples. In vain did Charles call the attention of his parents to the fact that Elbridge had been apparently a confirmed inebriate, and that any regimen, cooling to the system, and interdicting spirit,

would probably have cured him. Fruitlessly did he
plead that no good argument could be drawn from
such an instance, to prove that the same treatment
would be beneficial in a case like Delia's. The
young invalid herself was perfectly passive during
the deliberations. She had no thought of mental
independence. She chose to be led by others.
Had she occupied the position of Queen Catherine
Parr, when her life was in danger, she would have
made no attempt to conciliate the king, to remove
the unjust suspicions which had been fostered in
his mind by her enemies, but would have ignomini-
ously perished, like two of the former wives of the
royal Blue Beard. I will not say that Delia might
not have made a more noble character, or that she
was yet so far sunk in lethargy that she could not
now attain the eminence designed by nature for a
rightly directed mind of her caliber.

Charles, as usual, desired Adelaide's opinion.
She replied, that so great was her reverence for cold
water, that she inclined more favorably to this system than to any other. She had, however, so little
confidence in any kind of medical treatment, that
she should resort to it only in rare cases. She believed that health was the natural condition of the
human constitution, that disease was caused by a
violation of its laws, and that the normal state
might generally be regained by a return to obedience. She regarded hydropathy as the safest of
the extra modes of treatment. She felt confident

that many invalids had been essentially benefited by the cold-water practice. Hydropathy was now beginning to attract the attention of educated men, and, to an establishment conducted by one of those, she should not hesitate to resort in any case of emergency. But, whatever hydropathy might accomplish in many cases, it would probably be far from serviceable in Delia's. Her constitution was now so miserably weak, that it could hardly be deemed capable of the reaction requisite for obtaining any benefit from the sudden and prolonged application of large quantities of cold water.

In view of these statements, Charles advised his parents to wait awhile, until further inquiry could be made. In reply to this counsel, his mother indignantly asked whether he wished them to delay till his sister was irrecoverably ill. Charles knew that the plan would be negatived by every allopathic physician. What, then, could be done but to listen to the extravagant stories of Mr. Elbridge, and to read the enthusiastic reports of the hydropathists? A whole evening was spent in the perusal of Bulwer's eulogistic letter. All listened with wonder at the account of literary labor so severe and so unremitting, that at length not a day passed without its concomitants, pain and lassitude. Triumphant were their exclamations as they heard of the futile efforts of the allopathists. When Charles was reading the following passage, " We ransack the ends of the earth for drugs and minerals—we extract our potions from the deadliest poisons—but around us and about us Nature, the great mother, proffers the Hygeian fount, unsealed and accessible to all. Wherever the stream glides pure, wherever the spring sparkles fresh, there, for the vast proportion of the maladies which art produces, Nature yields the benignant healing"—every one felt an instantaneous desire for an immediate experience of the renovating effects of the great restorer.

James proposed three cheers for the "hydropathic romancer." Ella suggested an amendment to her brother's motion, by substituting the words "romancing hydropathist." Before the children could carry their plan into execution, they were silenced by their mother, who dryly remarked that she did not care to have her "parlor turned into a caucus." The discussion of hydropathy was again renewed. It shone in brilliant colors to the imagination of those who had been listening to Bulwer's sparkling epistle.

The document had been read on one of the warmest evenings of July. The Thorntons, in their enthusiasm, could not refrain from fancying that the fabled life of the Nereids was the most beautiful that could be conceived, and that, to be true hydropathists, they ought, indeed, to make their abode in the life-giving element. Even Delia began to feel some degree of interest in the anticipated marvels of the Water-Cure. Now, the excursion must be planned, and extensive preparations made for a long journey. The idea of going to the metropolis was abandoned. They had the discernment to perceive that the full advantages of hydropathy could be received only in a rural establishment. The institution located in the pleasant town of —— was, therefore, selected as the one most likely to confer all the benefits of the system.

Great indecision was manifested when the subject of Delia's traveling companion was presented. Who should accompany her? Mrs. Thornton bitterly regretted that Georgie was yet in the early stages of infancy. Not being weaned, he could not, of course, be left, even for the sake of her favorite Delia. To take him with her was also inadmissible; for how could she attend both to her nursing infant and her invalid daughter! No one was willing to trust Delia with only a domestic for a companion. A lady was indispensable. All thought, as Charles did, of his friend at the cottage. Would Adelaide, who, as Ella declared, was the impersonation of Addison's Fidelia, leave her father? Would she consent to go with Delia? Charles asserted that Captain Wilmot's health had lately improved to such a degree, that some hope was entertained of his partial recovery; that Adelaide, with all her other exploits, had made Rose as accomplished a nurse as herself, and that, if some companion could be found for the younger sister during the absence of the elder, their wishes would probably be gratified. Ella, with beaming eyes, begged that she might be allowed to stay with Captain Wilmot and Rose. In consequence of ill health, Miss Adams had appointed the vacation six weeks earlier than usual. Nothing would be more delightful than to work and study with Rose. Charles warmly advocated this plan. Mr. Thornton could not bear the thought of parting with Ella even for a few weeks. Mrs. Thornton, although perfectly willing to send the lawless child from home, did not quite like the idea of permitting her to visit the Wilmots. Both parents thought, however, that in gratitude to Adelaide, if she should consent to accompany Delia, they ought not only to spare Ella, but also to send a char-woman two or three days every week, to perform the heaviest part of the household labor. This plan formed, all were impatient till Adelaide's answer could be received. The self denying girl at first thought it impossible; but, her father so perseveringly urged the measure, saying that, besides gratifying the Thorntons, she would herself derive benefit from the journey, after toiling so steadily for him year after year. Adelaide replied that her life, during the time specified, had been one of great enjoyment. She had learned her own power. Both body and mind had been invigorated by the efforts which she had been compelled to make. But she would cheerfully comply with his wish, especially as provision so ample had been made for his comfort during her absence.

It was then arranged that Charles should escort

the two girls to ——, return immediately to his duties as teacher, and go for them when the time allotted for their stay had elapsed. This scheme was presently nullified. Those potent personages, the members of the school committee, proclaimed that no holydays could be allowed unless appointed by themselves.

Charles, despite his usual equanimity, seriously thought of sending in his resignation. But Adelaide remonstrated, that she did not think it right, for so trivial a cause, to abandon pupils who were now fairly under his influence.

An appeal was then made by Delia to her good, quiet father. He uttered a groan of despair. How could he take a long journey? He declared that he had accomplished no feat of the kind since the occasion of his marriage; when, in order to gratify his wife's wish to be considered fashionable, he had allowed her to drag him from a pleasant room, an easy walk, and the dreamy pleasure of examining his day-book and ledger, to the exciting joys of the coach, the canal, and the steamboat. Looking around for relief, he was, for the first time, impressed by the idea that, if Delia had had a lover, his services would have been very acceptable at this juncture. He averred that Ralph Waldo Emerson never made a more sensible remark than when he called *traveling, the fool's paradise.*

Adelaide, who saw his distress, playfully told him to banish it without delay, asserting that she

had not once thought of his taking the trouble to
be their escort; that she should not be afraid to go
from one end of the civilized world to the other
without a gentleman; that she did not regard the
protection of a male companion as at all requisite.
What more could a man do than a woman in the
matter of securing passages, ordering dinners, and
fastening trunks? Men might be of some use in a
savage country, where defensew as needed against
robbers and wild beasts; but in a land like this,
their aid was not essential, except in severe toil, such
as hewing forests and building houses. All labor,
except that requiring mere physical strength, could
be performed as well by women.

Mr. Thornton and Charles quite agreed with all
Adelaide's propositions. But, when Dr. Leland
chanced to hear of them, he shook his head, and
said that he should advise the young man not to
marry a woman so independent as Adelaide, who
would not concede that the sex to which God had
given the supremacy was superior to her own, except in physical strength. With a quiet smile,
Charles replied that he would receive the clergyman's lecture with due deference, and depute Adelaide to answer the charges made, and to defend the
opinions denounced.

One pleasant summer morning, Adelaide and her
charge left home in the cumbrous stage-coach,
which ran daily for the accommodation of the
Clintonians   Their quiet town had not been favored

by the introduction of those iron roads which, in
the multiplicity of their ramifications, have, as
some one has wittily observed, transformed the surface of our country into a vast gridiron. No bar
of this great national utensil had yet crossed Clinton. In the stage-coach, therefore, without a single
wish for a swifter mode of conveyance, the two
girls seated themselves, leaving behind them faces
as sanguine as if the fair travelers had been going
in quest of the fountain of perennial youth.

Three days afterward, a short letter was received,
doubtless written immediately before the departure
of the mail. Adelaide wrote that they should reach
their destination the next morning, and that the invalid, although fatigued by the journey, exhibited
no alarming symptoms of ill health. Delia added
a postscript, communicating the important information that the cooking at the hotels was not always
in the best style. Several times, however, Adelaide
had been so kind as to make biscuits, custards, and
raspberry jam, in their own room, so that she had
not suffered for the want of home comforts. Charles
sent to Adelaide a long letter, of which I shall give
no account; and to Delia, a short one, gently
chiding her for deporting so like an epicure. He
told her that she was a most miserable traveler, not
to be content with the common fare provided for
those who voluntarily leave their own culinary ac-
commodations, to encounter the varied experience
of the roving multitude, breakfasting, perchance,

at a metropolitan hotel, dining at an unpretending farm-house, and supping at a primitive log cabin.

A week elapsed without further tidings from the wanderers. Both families began to feel some degree of disquietude. Their anxiety was soon terminated. One day, as all the Thorntons were on a visit at Captain Wilmot's, the door suddenly opened, and in walked the two young ladies, with as much ease and composure as if they had only been rambling leisurely through the town. The expression of Adelaide's countenance could not be deciphered. Delia, although in good humor, was evidently mortified by some circumstance, and disposed to elude observation. After a few moments of exclamatory intercourse, an elucidation of the mystery was eagerly demanded. Delia half smiled and referred her friends to Adelaide, who briefly said that they reached Mr. Thornton's an hour previous, learned that the whole family were at Captain Wilmot's, removed their traveling dresses, and arrayed themselves for a walk to the cottage.

" But why have you returned so soon ?" cried Ella.

" Yes, yes, tell us why," echoed half a dozen voices.

" Give us the history of your adventures," called Captain Wilmot.

Adelaide smiled and looked at Delia, who slightly colored, but motioned for her to proceed.

" Adelaide must be weary," expostulated Charles, " we can wait till another day."

"I am perfectly well," replied Adelaide, "and quite ready to give you the desired explanation. Before consulting Dr. Lloyd, the hydropathic physician, we visited several of his patients, and asked as many questions as they would answer. Very many appeared content with the treatment, and confident that they should soon regain their health. Others complained that they were never before so ill. Dr. Lloyd had, however, told them that they must not expect to feel well till they had taken the whole course. I was much impressed by the general aspect of the patients. The habit of moderate exercise, the absence of dietic stimulants, and the frequent application of cold water, had, as it were, calmed all undue nervous excitement, entirely lulled passion, and substituted a species of serenity admirably adapted to promote convalescence."

"Why," interrupted Ella, "are the hydropathists strict with regard to the diet of their patients?"

"Indeed they are," replied Adelaide, with a mischievous glance at Delia. "The homeopathic rules are quite liberal when compared with these. The true hydropathist will allow no beverage but pure water. Narcotics, and condiments of every description, are forbidden. The patient may not even eat salt. The remaining dietetic regulations are such as would be sanctioned by all good physicians."

"Do the patients ever rebel?" inquired Mr. Thornton.

It was observed that Delia had suddenly become very much interested in twining the honeysuckles, which had partially escaped from their trellis, with the intention of climbing through the window. Adelaide smiled, and resumed, "An elderly gentleman, who had long been troubled with gout, resolved to try the Water-Cure. He reached —— the day previous to our arrival. For a week, he was tolerably compliant. He took douches and abreibungs in profusion, but always groaned when his simple meals were placed before him. Finally, he declared that, not even with the hope of permanent relief, could he submit to the bill of fare. Immediately before our departure, I saw him carefully lifted into his carriage by two servants. His face was purple, and his feet studiously bandaged."

"Oh, the gourmand!" exclaimed Ella.

"Do, Adelaide," demanded Captain Wilmot, "define those hard words which you used. Douches and the other one."

"Those are names of baths. I may as well give you the entire list. The *douche* is a stream of water descending upon the patient. This, although apparently simple, demands great caution. In some complaints, its administration would be attended with fatal consequences. The *abreibung* is a coarse, wet sheet, wrung a little, and thrown around the body. Warmth must be produced by friction. The *lein-tuch* is the simple wet sheet. The patient must be warm when it is applied. It is renewed more or less frequently according to the nature of the malady. *Umschlags* are bandages to act upon any part of the body as the lein-tuch does upon the whole. They are good for some local diseases. The *abgeschreckte* is a tepid bath. The *sitz* is a sitting bath. All these, and several others, are in constant use at the institution."

"Madame de Sévigné," observed Charles, "refers to the douche with horror. Was it the same kind of bath now employed by hydropathists?"

"The difference was in the temperature. Cold water was not then in favor. The hot-water douche was given to the accomplished letter-writer.

"The most important circumstance connected with the Water-Cure is the *crisis*. One lady, who had not taken the precaution to learn the principles of hydropathy, was very much alarmed by the appearance of numerous boils. Dr. Lloyd congratulated his terrified patient, assuring her that they denoted a favorable change, and, that she might now expect a thorough cure. Various explanations are given to account for the crisis. Sir Charles Scudamore sums up a series of remarks upon this subject, by saying, 'It is very evidently the formation of an artificial disease, with the hope that it may be a substitute for the real one, and cause its removal.' This doctrine seems to agree with some of those taught by the allopathists.

"Being much encouraged by the reports of the patients, Delia felt no repugnance to a consultation with the hydropathist. I gave him the history of her case. He asked a few questions, examined her with great attention, and frankly said that hers was one of the few cases requiring great caution in the application of hydropathy. He doubted not, however, but that, with care on his part, and attention on her own, she would soon derive essential benefit. The *sweating blanket* was first ordered. I will refer you to herself for the description."

Delia slightly shuddered. She would have refused compliance, had she not been desirous of gaining the sympathy of all present, that they might not blame her, on learning the sequel of the story. With a faint smile, she began, "I was placed upon a very hard mattress, and enveloped in a great number of blankets. I was so closely packed in these, that I could think of nothing, save the man in the iron shroud, on the seventh morning of his imprisonment. A burning fever soon ensued. Cold bandages were then applied to my head, but not one of the heavy blankets was removed. After awhile, the disagreeable sensations ceased. Copious perspiration gave relief. I was directed to drink as much cold water as I could. After this treatment had been pursued till I was nearly exhausted, I was taken out, and rubbed with wet cloths. This bath was repeated several times during my stay. Adelaide will tell you what followed."

With heightened curiosity, the auditors turned toward Adelaide. "Delia," resumed Adelaide, "pa-

tiently took the baths, and observed the dietetic
rules for three days. Then, being, as she afterward confessed, half-famished, she eat freely of
sundry cakes and other delicacies, which, unknown
to me, she had secreted in her trunk. Perceiving
by her symptoms that his rules had been disregarded, Dr. Lloyd compelled her to acknowledge the
fact, and dismissed her from the institution."

"I declare," ejaculated Mrs. Thornton, trotting
Georgie so energetically that his face soon gave
premonition of rapidly impending convulsions,
"how much Delia has to suffer!"

Mr. Thornton was silent. Charles quietly observed, "Delia should have refrained from eating the
forbidden fruit."

"She was hungry," pleaded Rose.

"But she should have obeyed orders," said Captain Wilmot; "my sailors never ventured to violate
a command. I wonder at Delia's presumption."

"What kind of a man is Dr. Lloyd?" asked Ella,
with the benevolent design of diverting the general
attention from her sensitive sister.

"He is quite tall and large," replied Adelaide,
"and his countenance looks as if he every day read
Foster's 'Essay on Decision of Character.' He
walks around with an air of inflexible severity, and
delivers his orders without appearing to imagine
that a law enacted by him might be disregarded.
Napoleon would not allow that *impossible* was a
French word. Dr. Lloyd evidently intends to ex-

clude it from the English language. He thinks
that almost every disease may be cured by hydropathy, although he admits that, in some cases,
great caution is required in its administration."

"Would he say," inquired Charles, "that he
could cure consumption ?"

"His pretensions would exceed those of a large
majority of physicians. They all maintain that,
except in the very first stages, this fearful malady
is incurable. Who, indeed, can reasonably anticipate the recovery of a person thus seriously diseased ? But, Dr. Lloyd says that ulcers in the
lungs may sometimes be healed as well as in any
other part of the body."

"Do you believe that doctrine, Adelaide ?"

"I will answer by asking another question. Do
you remember what Dr. Perry said of Mrs. Allen ?"

"Oh, yes, but I had forgotten. She was out of
health for years. Nor is she now perfectly well.
The physician long since pronounced her complaint
to be pulmonary consumption. A few months ago,
a change in her symptoms induced him to propose
a consultation. Two distinguished physicians met
with him for the purpose of an examination. They
published, as the result, that her case was one of a
thousand. After suffering frightful laceration by
disease, her lungs had partially healed. They asserted, however, that no encouragement could, from
this instance, be given to patients affected with
consumption. Hers was a case of rare occur-

rence, acting merely as an exception to prove the rule."

"That was the statement. Although my opinion is not quite formed, I can not wholly avoid the inference, that what was effected on this occasion, by causes unknown to us, may again be witnessed. Still, it is preposterous to hope that a case of confirmed consumption could be cured. Only an empiric would assert that a person thus seriously diseased could ever enjoy sound health."

Mrs. Thornton, who never ventured to let Georgie be away from home in the evening, now plainly announced, that preparations for their immediate departure must be made. These always occupied many minutes, for, even at the time of the summer solstice, the tender mother would carefully envelope the poor child in hood, tippet, and cloak. To complete his traveling costume, mittens were thrust upon his little hands, and an almost impervious green veil drawn over his face. On a former occasion, Adelaide had gently intimated, that his constitution could not be more effectually enfeebled than by a superabundance of warm clothing. In reply to this hint, Mrs. Thornton had angrily exclaimed, " Adelaide Wilmot, do you suppose that you know more about babies than the mother of eleven children ?"

Adelaide, on being thus addressed, had longed to say, that the little graves of the deceased infants would never have been filled, had their mother studied and practised the laws of physiology. But she had thought it wiser to refrain. She now also stood in silence, merely pitying the child as he sent up one faint cry for the pure air of which his mother was depriving him. Georgie was finally equipped, and deposited, like a bale of merchandise, in the baby-carriage, which was standing at the door. Ella assumed the office of conductor, and stood playing bo-peep with the little prisoner through his green veil, while the "last words" were exchanged by the others.

XII.

LIFE.

"In the world's broad field of battle,
In the bivouac of Life,
Be not like dumb, driven cattle!
Be a hero in the strife!"—LONGFELLOW.

"WHAT shall we do for you, my poor Delia?" said Mr. Thornton, anxiously gazing upon the pale countenance of his invalid child.

"Let me die, papa," replied the young lady, in a half-angry, half-plaintive tone, "I have no wish to live."

The father's eyes distended with as much horror as the mildness of his character would allow.

"So young, and yet you have no wish for a continuance of the boon of life. My dear child, you must be very ill, or you would not feel thus. Life, even with its trials, is a state of happiness. How much we all enjoy! I am frequently oppressed by the cares of business, and annoyed by the uncontrolled passions of those by whom I am surrounded, but still, in view of the amount of bliss received from other sources, I would not lose a single day which I have passed on earth."

The good man folded his hands in silent gratitude. Charles and Adelaide had entered while he was speaking. They looked at each other with eyes of eloquence. What was conveyed in that mute address? Unuttered words, I fancy, to this effect:

"If life is good to him, with his quiet temperament, how rich, how ecstatic, must it be to those of more intense feelings, of greater capacities for thought, of more vigorous powers of action!"

"I know," resumed Mr. Thornton, "that life is sometimes considered a burden by those who are in ill health, but, if the question of its abandonment were seriously asked, would the response be affirmative? During my severe illness last winter, I suffered greatly from pain and languor. But, in my quiet intervals, in my hours of comparative comfort, my thoughts were very pleasant. I reclined upon my couch, enjoying the pleasures of reverie. Life appeared desirable, were it merely for the enjoyment conferred by the sense of existence."

"My father," observed Adelaide, "in the midst of his severest sufferings, has often said, 'Life is beautiful, my children. I should be sorry to die, even were I quite confident of a transition to a nobler state of being.' Yet, is it not strange, that those whose life must be one of almost incessant pain, should so desire to live?"

"Because, Adelaide," returned Charles, "of the uncertain future. Whither do we go on quitting this beautiful earth?"

"One would infer, Charles, that you were an unbeliever."

"Not so, Adelaide. The evidences of Christianity are unerring. The truths of revelation may be received by every humble heart. But, who has returned from the dread world to which we are hastening? My faith is only faith. Strong as it occasionally is, it can not be called sight. Therefore, I should cling to earth, even if I were enduring the extreme of misery."

"Here I must agree with Dr. Leland, that moral demonstration is as conclusive as mathematical. Faith in its infancy is doubtless feeble; otherwise, it might be termed presumption. But, after years of trust and experience, may not every Christian say, with Paul, ' I know in whom I have believed?' "

"Those only who reach that state can be considered truly happy. All others, those who merely doubt, as well as those who disbelieve, must be more or less unhappy."

"Children," said Mr. Thornton, with a troubled brow, "you are contradicting yourselves. A few minutes since, you maintained that all were happy."

"No, sir," replied Adelaide, "that was not our exact position. We merely assumed that the love of life was inherent in every one, despite the personal misery which each might endure."

"I will not subscribe even to that doctrine," remarked Delia. "If it were true, why should any one commit suicide?"

"I doubt whether any sane person would be guilty of that act, or would even indulge the thought of self-destruction."

"Adelaide," exclaimed Delia, her voice trembling with unwonted energy, "you are too happy ever to dream of such a thought. Your study has been extensive, your observation close, and your experience varied. But you are not competent to judge of what passes in the hearts of those who are wretched without the ability to explain the cause of their sufferings. Some say that your lot has been hard, but they do not perceive the truth. Labor has been assigned you, but, with your views, it could not be deemed a burden. You have had time for your favorite pursuit, study; and you have found some one whom you could love with all the strength of which your affections are susceptible. You should not profess to understand subjects on which you have had no experience. You have endured nothing to elicit the thought,

> "'O that the Everlasting had not fixed
> His canon 'gainst self-slaughter!'"

Delia would have proceeded further, but her utterance was impeded by a violent paroxysm of tears. Fear pervaded the hearts of her auditors, but not more than they had felt from the very commencement of her remarks. It was unusual for Delia to attempt any thing like a regular harangue. Her habits, both of thought and of action, were opposed to the expression of more than a few words at a

time. Her hearers had, therefore, listened with
consternation, as she delivered sentence after sentence, in so frenzied a manner. All now united in
entreating her to retire to her own room. Her nervous system, they argued, had been so excited that
she was in absolute need of repose. But, controlling herself by a violent effort, she said that it was
her wish to remain. After an awkward pause, she
calmly requested them to pursue the conversation.
With one glance of fearful scrutiny toward his
sister, Charles said, in reply to her previous remarks,
"The problem is not yet solved, Delia, whether a
person is capable of describing well what he has
never experienced. Adelaide will not assert that
she has the power. In her humility, she would
probably deny that in her mind it exists to any
extent. I firmly believe that she is largely endowed
with this rare gift. Do you remember the criticism
of the great essayist, Giles, on the anecdote of Byron
and the dagger? As the poet held the deadly
weapon, he longed to know how a man must feel
after committing murder. According to the critic,
Byron needed the actual experience of an event, in
order to give a faithful description. Shakspeare,
he intimates, could understand all passions, and
express every shade of feeling, and each act of the
soul, with no real prototype in his own mental or
bodily deeds. This was in consequence of his un-
rivalled creative power."

Adelaide blushed painfully, and Delia made no

attempt to repress her smiles.   Mr. Thornton glanced mischievously toward the young lady who was the indirect subject of this eulogy, and said, in a tone of raillery, "You ought to thank me for my son, Adelaide.   He thinks that you have power comparable to Shakspeare's."

"I do not regard a flatterer as a gift deserving of the least gratitude," replied Adelaide, with more indignation than she had ever before exhibited.

"But," pleaded Charles, "I wished to convince Delia that you could understand her position without her experience;" then, abruptly turning to his sister, he asked, "If you were as well as Adelaide, would not life be acceptable?"

With an arch smile, the young girl answered, "I can not imagine such a case.   I must acknowledge myself Byronian rather than Shaksperian.   I can not conceive of any act, of any state of being, emotion, or even sensation, without personal experience of the same."

"Delia," exclaimed Mr. Thornton, "don't be metaphysical.   I do not know what you mean.   You have so long been silent, that we must learn your language."

"You need not fear, papa; I am entirely devoid of metaphysical talent."

"You are wretched, Delia.   Can you tell us what would render you happy?   What would inspire you with that love of life which is so natural to the human race?"

Delia shook her head, and answered, "I can not concede that life is either beautiful or desirable. I should be willing to die, were it not for the dread of what Charles calls the 'uncertain future.'"

All slightly shuddered. It was sad to see the pall of grief o'ershadowing one who had known so little of the real anguish which is, at some stage, the lot of all those who have long trodden the journey of life.

"Why, Delia," inquired Adelaide, "should you recoil from the idea of death? Charles alleges weakness of faith as his reason."

"Mine is total want of faith. The ancient Pagan idea of the future world occupies my mind far more than that held by you and other Christians. We are told that those with whom the gods were not personally offended, were engaged in the unreal performance of the same acts that had engrossed their attention during life. May not this be true? Is it not probable that Charles will teach in heaven? Will not Adelaide zealously study the language of the immortals, and also administer to those who, although glorified in Paradise, will need the assistance of the strong in mind? May not our neighbors have employments resembling those which they have pursued in this world? We are taught by Christianity that this life is a state of preparation for the next. Do not the two systems here coincide? Shall we not, in heaven, labor in such departments as we have qualified ourselves for on earth?"

"What employment have you assigned for yourself?" asked Adelaide, with deep interest.

"Oh, I am one of those who have offended the gods. My life has been useless. I shall be excluded from the home of the 'good and faithful.' In the prison of the wretched, I shall live as I have on earth, listless and suffering, with a constant accession of pain."

"Delia, Delia!" cried her father, "cease raving. You are distracting us all."

"Adelaide," queried Delia, with that restless manner which betrays agitation that can not be controlled, "what is the cause of happiness in this life?"

"Obedience," was Adelaide's prompt answer, as she gazed compassionately upon the trembling girl.

"Obedience!" echoed Delia, impatiently, "obedience to whom?"

"Obedience to God, that is, to the laws which He has made. Laws have been justly called 'expressions of the thoughts of God.' Edicts have been proclaimed for all mankind. The natural law, which is written upon the heart even of the savage. The moral law, which is in accordance with the natural. Rules were given for the observance of the disciples of Christ. Did not Locke regard the 'Sermon on the Mount,' as a summary of directions for those who should enlist under the banner of Jesus? Then, too, we have laws for the preservation of health. We are as culpable for willful disregard of these, as for actual violation of the direct injunctions of the decalogue. God has revealed the organic laws to those who have made the subject their study."

"How then can any one be happy? All have broken the law."

"True. Perfect happiness can not therefore be enjoyed in this life. Only an approximation to such a state can be expected. The consciousness of pardon for past errors, implicit confidence in the promises of our Saviour, and a constant strife for perfect obedience, are the only pure sources of happiness."

Delia sighed. "This never-ceasing effort seems hard."

"We are told that it is hard. To what is the Christian life compared? To the races of the ancients, which required the exercise of all the vigor possessed by the competitors. But, you are not well enough to bear any longer the excitement of conversation. Let us join the children."

XIII.

HIC HOMO ET HÆC HOMO.

"God made him, and therefore let him pass for a man."—SHAKSPEARE.

A VERY faint ring, of the apologetic species, was, one fine evening, heard at Mr. Thornton's door. Surely at no time previous had bell been so gently handled. Ella half-smiled, curled her lip, did profound obeisance to the yet unseen comer, and said, "Sir, or madam, I forgive you with all my heart."

The words had hardly escaped, when Dora ushered into the room a gentleman, who had come, as he himself announced, to spend a "sociable evening."

With one sigh of submission to their fate, the Thorntons invited their visitor to be seated. The reason of the sigh will be learned with one glance at the character of the man.

The expression of Mr. Stanson's countenance was very humble, as he thought; but, very abject, as every intelligent reader of physiognomy declared. Although an uneducated man, he had, in consequence of several peculiarities in our social system, gained no unenviable position in the society of his native town. His purse received the homage which was denied to his brain.

By virtue of his manhood, he was entitled to the exercise of the elective franchise. His vote was always given for the man approved by Squire Hughes and Dr. Leland. Had these two vanes pointed in different directions, the bewildered Stanson would have failed to discern that the political horizon could ever again regain its wonted serenity. But, as he had always been taught to obey Dr. Leland, he would have done so in this case. He would also have relieved any doubt of the clergyman's infallibility, by arguing that the learned lawyer had probably been hired by government. Even Demosthenes, as Stanson once said, on a similar occasion, accepted a bribe from Harpalus. Who these flagitious men were, or what was the bribe, or on what occasion it was offered, or whether the renowned orator pleaded *guilty* to the charge, were questions which Mr. Stanson could not have answered. In town-meeting, he never hazarded a speech, but gave his vote as directed by the leaders of the prominent party. But, in the church or conference meeting, where, in accordance with Congregational usage, every man, however illiterate, is patiently allowed to have a place in the debates, he only waited to see which side would be advocated by the clergyman. When, at the close of a stormy discussion, he was personally called upon for an expression of his mind, he replied, in subdued accents, " I agree with the pastor." The young men and maidens who had been gathered into the bosom of the church, could not always repress their inclination to smile when Brother Stanson's opinion was asked. Their elders, however, preserved a state of decorum as remarkable as it was exemplary. In matters of state, as I have intimated, he never spoke, deeming the republic safe, if he voted with the greatest men of Clinton. But, in a religious meeting, he was sometimes tempted to display his power. His exhortation was then a repetition, in feeble language, and distorted signification, of the sentiments conveyed in a previous address of some one of the brethren of the church. His prayers were beyond description. The most rigid Congregationalists, if they could claim any spark of intelligence, did, for the moment, long for some "excellent liturgy." Adelaide, conscientiously forbearing to join in his petitions, silently prayed that the time might soon come when women of talent and education should take part in the public services of religion; and when men devoid of both natural and acquired ability to instruct their brethren and sisters, should be compelled to maintain silence.

Was it surprising, then, that his visits were in demand only among those of his own caliber?

"Well, how do you all do?" drawled the intruder, as he ensconced his meager frame amid the sofa cushions, from which, on perceiving his intention, Carrie had retreated in dire dismay.

"Quite well, thank you, except Delia," replied Mr. Thornton, with a regretful glance at the newspaper, as he deposited it upon the table.

"What is the matter with you, Delia?" asked Mr. Stanson; "every body is talking about your health."

Delia, who, despite her foibles, detested a sympathetic cross-examination, differing, in this respect, from those inconsiderate invalids who are continually obtruding their ailments upon the notice of their friends, replied, "Do not distress yourself, sir, I am very well."

At which incredible statement, every one in the room looked at the young lady with a comic affectation of amazement.

"Delia," said Stanson, shaking his insignificant head, in a manner intended to be very impressive, and poising his forefinger upon some invisible object suspended in the air, "I am fairly astonished. You are not speaking the truth. Have your parents never taught you the ninth commandment? You look as if you were in the last stage of consumption. My niece, who died last fall of that terrible disease, was not so much emaciated as you are. You ought to be edifying yourself with thoughts of grave-yards and tomb-stones."

Ella, although she had been told a thousand times, that whispering in company was a heinous offense against the laws of etiquette, murmured to her sister, "Don't faint, Delia. Let him talk. He reminds me of that self-complacent Malvolio, who believed that ' he had greatness thrust upon him.'"

"Mr. Thornton, with as much alacrity as his mental habits would allow, said, "My good sir, you mistake. My daughter did not design to prevaricate. She feels well this evening."

"Ay, ay," ejaculated the tormentor, "consumption is a very flattering disease!"

Mrs. Thornton could no longer attend to the terrific chasm in Jamie's jacket, which had for the last half hour demanded the exercise of all the skill of which her needle was capable. Like an avalanche, did her words fall upon the ear of her guest. "I should like to know, sir, whether you have come to my house for the express purpose of murdering my daughter. Her nervous system is highly excitable. If I wanted to kill her, I should talk in that style."

"I beg pardon, madam," stammered Stanson, looking askance at his hostess.

"Delia, my love," said Mrs. Thornton, without noticing the petition, "you have been up a long time. You must retire early this evening."

"Pray, mamma, permit me to remain," was the laughing response of Delia, who was too well aware of Stanson's ignorance on all subjects, to be alarmed by any prognostication which he might attempt.

"How is Mrs. Stanson?" inquired Mr. Thornton, solicitous to introduce another topic, "and why did not she come with you?"

"Mrs. Stanson's health is very poor," answered the gentleman, his head again giving that ominous, oscillatory movement; "she won't be here long. She never goes out evenings."

The actual truth was, that Mrs. Stanson, having, like many another woman, married a man greatly her inferior, found his presence so intolerable that, under various pretexts, she continually avoided his society, never visiting with him when she could devise any excuse for remaining at home, and always resolutely refusing to invite company to her own domicile. That her cheeks might not every day tingle with shame on account of his ignorance and stupidity, she led, as far as she could, a separate life, and spent a good part of her time in studying those authors who have expatiated upon the subject of Divorce.

Stanson now heaved a sigh, so deeply resonant that it might be termed cavernous, and drew across his eyes a bandanna handkerchief, one of that frightful, sanguinary-hued description, which always seems to imply that the owner may have been committing murder.

"If Mrs. Stanson should die, and leave me solitary in the world, and my innocent children motherless, I should be called to suffer a great affliction. May I have strength to bear up under the trial!"

The widower, by anticipation, here assumed so lachrymose an appearance, that Ella found it politic to give close attention to her lesson.

"What are you studying, my dear?" inquired the visitor, with an air of condescension.

"Cæsar's Commentaries," was the laconic reply.

"I never heard of those commentaries. Our minister did not mention them when he was telling me how to study the Scriptures in the most profitable manner. Does Cæsar comment upon the Old or the New Testament?"

This was too much for Ella's gravity. She could not refrain from giving utterance to a shout of laughter. Mrs. Thornton's needle shot vehemently through Jamie's jacket. Mr. Thornton and Delia riveted their eyes upon a venerable Malta cat, the very personification of sobriety.

As soon as Mr. Thornton could venture to speak, he said, "At times, Ella is slightly hysterical. You were alluding, sir, to Dr. Leland—"

"Yes, yes, but those commentaries—what are they?"

Ella's eyes sparkled. Delia gave her an emphatic frown, but the eager child whispered, "If he will expose himself, let him," and then replied,

"Sir, these commentaries have no connection with the Bible. They were written by Cæsar, a celebrated Roman. They contain an account of a certain war, in which he greatly distinguished himself. The language is Latin."

Stanson's face was a perfect blank.

"I never studied that language," was his candid confession.

"Of course, you never did," muttered impertinent little Ella.

"Such studies are of no use," continued the despiser of human learning; "Dr. Leland would not approve of them."

"Sir, you know nothing about the matter. It is the language of the learned world. No one ignorant of Latin can claim the proud title of scholar. Dr. Leland would not be a respectable clergyman without an aquaintance with the very language which you condemn."

Stanson shrank into his corner, and meekly said, "I hope that you find your book interesting."

"On the contrary, sir, although Latin is my favorite study, this is the dullest book which I ever read. The only interesting part is a description of the early inhabitants of Britain. I am studying Cæsar, that I may be qualified for the perusal of the larger classics. I shall soon begin the Latin poets. Those will be fascinating. By-and-by, I shall pass on to Greek, which my brother Charles says is incomparably superior to Latin."

Stanson elevated both hands and eyes.

"Strange that a pious woman, like Miss Adams, should make her scholars study heathen books."

"Sir, those heathen books, as you call them, are studied by all Christians who receive a liberal education. Our clergymen pursue the regular course, or they would not be deemed fit for their office."

"Do you mean that Dr. Leland has read books written by those pagans?"

"I do. He would not have ventured to apply for admission at a theological seminary, unless he had previously passed through an academic and a collegiate course."

"Sir," said the astonished Stanson, turning to Ella's father, "is your child speaking the truth?"

"Certainly, sir. A knowledge of the language and the literature of those polished nations of antiquity, is justly considered requisite for a leader of the people."

"I can not see how those men who worshiped idols could write any thing which could prepare a man to preach the gospel."

"You should not confound the Greeks and Romans with the degraded idolaters of our own times. The books which they wrote are without a parallel. Many even go so far as to say that genius left the world with Homer and Virgil. We should also remember, that, in addition to the direct benefit derived from such studies, the scholar gains an immense amount of mental discipline, which qualifies him, as perhaps nothing else would, for the wrestling that he must encounter as a good soldier of Christ. Without a thorough course of training, a man would be poorly prepared to defend the faith."

Stanson sat in silence, his brain almost turned by these ideas. His own deficiences had never before been so clearly revealed. At length he said, in a tone of pique, "I don't pretend to say that a man, especially a minister, does not need such studies, but, of what use can they be to a woman?"

Ella started from her seat, her eyes flashing, and her whole frame quivering with excitement. "Of the same use, Mr. Stanson, that they are to a man. They develop and discipline the mind. Every individual, endowed with mind, has a right to education. The fact that any man has a capacious mind, establishes his claim to high culture."

"Ay, a man, but not a woman!" said Stanson, bridling in his pride of sex.

"In Latin," replied Ella, with dignity, "*homo* may signify an individual of either sex. If I choose to employ the English word *man* in the same way, you can not dispute my right. You are not a philologist."

Stanson, who had experienced more or less of discomfort for the last few minutes, and who did not, indeed, understand the meaning of Ella's last sentence, was inexpressibly relieved on hearing an energetic peal of the door-bell. A moment after Dr. Leland, in his genial, but almost pontifical humor, entered the room.

Ella leaped from the music-stool, on which she had been perched, and met the clergyman with a joyful grasp of the hand. The senior Thorntons advanced with respectful cordiality. Stanson, meanwhile, stood in silence, achieving most extraordinary prostrations. He would fain have touched the carpet with his forehead, had his limbs possessed the requisite pliancy. On seeing him, Dr. Leland, in his effort to suppress an involuntary laugh, was attacked by one of his alarming paroxysms. After coughing till his lungs fairly ached, he smiled, and glanced around the room, carefully averting his eyes from Stanson, who, overwhelmed with a consciousness of the pastor's proximity, was sitting with downcast eyes and folded hands, looking as some good Romanist might in the presence of the Pope. Even the President of the Republic would have received no more homage from Stanson than did our much-amused clergyman. Dr. Leland did, indeed, consider himself as the equal of any man, not excepting the most distinguished, but the curious manifestations of deference which he was obliged to endure from some of his parishoners, were almost too much for the due maintenance of his gravity.

"Dr. Leland," demanded Ella, without waiting for conventionalisms, "should not women be permitted to study the classics?"

"Who denies them the privilege?" asked the gentleman, with a smile.

"In my youth," simpered Stanson, heartily wishing that the child were in bed, "little girls were told that they should be seen, and not heard."

"Why, Mr. Stanson," said the clergyman, with a

mock deprecatory air, " you would not compel our little friend to be a mere speechless automaton?"

Stanson, who was ignorant of the meaning of the last word, took refuge in silence.

The victor Ella continued, " Why, sir, Mr. Stanson has been saying that women ought not to learn Latin and Greek. Will you tell him that they should attend to every branch of study for which they have the talent?"

Dr. Leland laughed, and replied, " You have told him that, yourself, Ella. Will it not suffice?"

"No, no; he calls me a little girl. Do you tell him. He regards all that you say as *ex cathedra.*"

"Oh, you little pedant! Well, Mr. Stanson, I am commissioned by Miss Ella Thornton, to tell you that women have a right to study every thing for which they have the talent, even magic, Chaldee, and Japanese, if they aspire to topics of such interest."

"Now, say that your opinion agrees with mine."

" My opinion agrees with hers," repeated the reverend doctor, with great deliberation, as if he certainly knew his lesson, but chose to take due time for correct recitation.

Stanson, who had never learned, with Paley, that, " he who is not a fool half of the time, is a fool all the time ;" and who, moreover, had never heard of a certain eminent statesman's game of horses with his children, began to wonder what had become of his pastor's dignity. Like some other simple men, he always associated a long face, and a stern or dis-

mal countenance, with profound wisdom. The fear
now seized him, that Dr. Leland, his cherished oracle, was suddenly verging toward idiocy. This
supposition, however, he resolutely banished from
his mind. The effort to ponder upon its consequences was greater than he could well sustain. Hum-
bled by the clergyman's apparent acquiescence in
the views of Ella, he sank back upon the sofa in a
state of woful embarrassment, and fervently rejoiced
that Mrs. Stanson had been too ill to leave home that
evening. At length he summoned courage to ask,
in a trembling voice, " Do you think that women
should be lawyers and ministers ?"

"Ah! that is another question," replied the clergyman, releasing Ella's hand, and looking proudly
around the room, " a woman may study every thing
for which she has the time and the talent. You
would have figured better, Mr. Stanson, some cen-
turies before this age of the world. Many women,
with only a few advantages, have acquired great
erudition. How then can we deny that they have
the mental power to equal man in all his pursuits?
We must acknowledge that a woman may be whatever she chooses, in character and acquirements.
All, however, with the exception of a few ultraists,
agree that her position should be limited. Many a
man, in looking upon some noble woman, has felt
as did Shah Aulum, when he said, 'If Juliana
were a man, I would make him my vizier.' A
woman's mind should be cultivated, that she may

rightly fill her own sphere, not that she may en-
croach upon man's. I am entirely willing that my
wife should be my compeer in learning. But the
influence of her knowledge must bear upon her
children, and upon general society. She may benefit the world as much as she pleases, by teaching,
by conversation, and even by writing, but she shall
not enter the pulpit, or plead at the bar, or lecture
before any audience."

"Now you only half agree with me," said Ella,
with a shade upon her bright face.

"My dear child, how can you complain? Woman may well be content with the influence which
she can exert in private life. Far from resembling
the philosopher, who thanked Heaven that he was
not born a woman, I sometimes almost envy her
lot. In public, my influence extends over a thousand people. In private, it is not a tithe of that
possessed by my wife. The morals, the manners,
even the minds of my children, are formed wholly
by her. Very promising youth they are, but when
I look at one trait or another in their characters, I
remember that it was developed by their mother's
careful training and example. Not that an illiterate
woman would have had this power. But, being
highly educated, her sons and her daughters have
been inspired with reverence for her literary attainments as well as for her moral excellence. When
I married, people laughed at my learned wife, and
benevolently predicted that we should both come

upon the parish. As if a knowledge of the higher
branches of study precluded the idea of skill in domestic economy! Whose home is happier than my
own? Had it not been for my wife, I should have
become harshly bigoted, fiercely despotic. Her
refining influence has modified and rightly directed
the bias of my mind, so that I am not quite the
dogmatist for which I was fitted by the circumstances of my early life. She has been the sharer of my
cares and of my studies; she has educated my
children in the beauty of knowledge and of holiness;
she has been the loved companion of my leisure
hours. Oh, my dear Ella, how can woman complain that her sphere is circumscribed?"

Ella sighed. She was affected by the touching
eulogium which her pastor had given his wife, but
in more respects than one, was she dissatisfied with
the position occupied by the lady. She blushed,
and said, in a low tone, "But, you are the ruler."

"Not so, my child. Where the husband and the
wife are what they should be, a command is never
heard. Both obey the great laws promulgated by
the Sovereign of the Universe. People rule by
their influence. My wife's power with me is equal
to mine with her. When men are men, when, either
by the training of others, or by their own self-edu-
cation, they are what they should be, they always
acknowledge the sway of woman. Irresistibly do
they submit to her will. Both sexes are thus enno-
bled. You have read of Gorgo?"

"Gorgo!" repeated Ella, mournfully shaking her head, "no, sir."

"Time enough yet, my dear. I am sure that you have heard of Leonidas."

"Yes, indeed. Leonidas was king of Sparta."

"Right, and Gorgo was his wife. A foreign lady once said to the queen, 'You Spartan women are the only ones that rule men.' To which Gorgo replied, 'True, for we are the only ones that give birth to men.' The inference which I draw from this fine repartee might be thus expressed: Every man who is a true man evinces honor and reverence for woman. However much may be said to the contrary, woman does indeed rule man. She influences him, not only in his pliant childhood, his susceptible youth, but also in his proud maturity. As, in the days of chivalry, the chief motive to exertion would have been removed if woman, in her grace and beauty, had not been present to applaud the victors, and to crown them with the reward of their valor; so, now, if she were banished from our halls of public resort, from our social gatherings, how much of most powerful stimulus would vanish! How few would be so eager to display all their prowess in the contests of our mental knights!"

This rhetoric was thrown away upon the laughing child. She had not the most remote idea of "being flattered out of her rights."

"Do you think, sir, that women will be content as mere spectators? Instead of applauding and encouraging the men, we wish to be actors in the great drama of life."

The clergyman, unused to opposition, now appeared slightly vexed.

"Have I not indicated the way in which you are to act?" he demanded, with some degree of asperity.

"You have given me your views of our duty," replied Ella, with a mischievous smile, "but they do not satisfy me. I can not very well defend my own opinions. You should hear Adelaide."

"I have heard her," muttered Dr. Leland, with a dire contraction of his brow. After a pause, he resumed, "My child, you must be independent. Beware of yielding to the influence even of one so gifted as Adelaide."

"I am independent," replied Ella, proudly; "I should not accept an opinion from any one without due investigation."

"Remember, too, that your years on earth have been very few. You do not yet see objects in their true light."

Ella made no answer. She was endeavoring to recall a sentiment which she had somewhere seen, "Be true to the dream of thy youth."

Dr. Leland looked thoughtfully into Ella's earnest eyes, and continued,

"Adelaide's opinions upon some subjects are erroneous, but she may yet be convinced that she is wandering in devious paths. She is what I call a tangential young lady, if I may be allowed to coin a word."

The idea of comparing Adelaide with a tangent was so ludicrous, that Ella, for a moment, forgot the previous train of thought.

Dr. Leland proceeded. "I dislike ultraists. They would overturn the whole system of society, yea, the world itself, for the sake of their opinions."

"Have not all the reformers been ultraists?" asked Ella, with daring look and tone. "Was not Luther deemed an ultraist, by those who would have preferred to sleep quietly in error, rather than be rashly awaked?"

The clergyman playfully put his hand before Ella's mouth, saying, "That will do for this evening, child. I came to see your brother, not to hold an argument with you. Is he at home?"

"No, sir," answered Ella, with an arch smile, "he is at Adelaide's."

Dr. Leland's visage was slightly contorted, as he rose to depart. "When I next come, Ella, you shall not talk all the time. I shall see what your father and mother have to say. I must now find Charles."

All had forgotten Stanson. Ella, turning her head, saw her sanctimonious opponent completely lost in a state of somnolence. So many successive sentences uttered in the familiar tones of his pastor's voice had, by the laws of association, been as effectual a sedative as a sermon in the old church.

For the last quarter of an hour he had been under the dominion of Morpheus and his poppy-stalk Ella, with a suppressed laugh, directed the clergyman's attention to his interesting parishioner. Dr. Leland, with a significant nod, endeavored to creep noiselessly from the room. Vain attempt for a man encumbered with two hundred and fifty pounds of material substance! Stanson fairly awoke, yawned, and said, quite coherently, "Yes, yes, Miss Ella, I hope that you will remember what the minister has been saying to you this evening."

Another yawn, and he rose upon his feet. "Are you going, Dr. Leland? Wait a moment. I shall take the same road."

The persecuted clergyman gave a groan of assent. The next moment, accompanied by his presumptuous follower, he was groping his way through streets yet unfavored by gas or even oil. Clinton was never illumed except by Cynthia and her stellar train.

XIV.

SYMPATHY.

"God-written thoughts are in my heart,
And deep within my being lie,
Eternal truths and glorious hopes,
Which I must speak before I die."—GRACE GREENWOOD.

THAT night brought no refreshing sleep for the
excited Ella. She was disturbed by one feverish
dream after another, till, fairly exhausted, she rejoiced to see the first faint streaks which announced
the dawn. She rose, bathed, and dressed with unwonted languor, and then stood dizzily before the
open window, looking into the fair face of the sky,
as the stars gently vanished, and the clear summer
air kissed her throbbing brow.

"'I laid me down and slept; I awaked; for the
Lord sustained me.' No calm slumber have I had,
but I am grateful for life and for the sunrise,"
whispered the child, as she reverently knelt to offer
her morning prayer. She arose, and again looked
out upon the beautiful earth, repeating, as she did
so, Longfellow's exquisite "Hymn to the Night."
She had often risen with it upon her lips, and
sought to imbibe the tranquil radiance infused

through the poem. Now, when she came to the lines,

> "From the cool cisterns of the midnight air
> My spirit drank repose;"

she murmured, "I must rather say, with the wretched Clarence,

> "'O I have passed a miserable night,
> So full of fearful dreams, of ugly sights,
> That, as I am a Christian faithful man,
> I would not spend another such a night,
> Though 'twere to buy a world of happier days;
> So full of dismal terror was the time.'"

She descended to the parlor, opened her writing-desk, and began a theme required for the next day. She had been directed to note the points of resemblance and of discrepancy in the characters of Cleopatra and Elizabeth. She sat a few moments, trying to picture to herself, the "serpent of old Nile," and "the high and mighty princess of England." Before she had written a single paragraph, she was compelled by a violent headache, an unusual symptom in her, to lay aside her task. She put on her sun-bonnet, and sauntered, for she was too ill to walk with her habitual brisk step, to the little brown cottage of the Wilmots. She found Adelaide pacing the garden, evidently absorbed in thought.

"Ella!" exclaimed the astonished girl, "what has happened? Is Delia worse?"

"She was quite well last evening. Oh, Adelaide, if you had only been at our house!"

"You are mysterious this morning. Should I have been glad or sorry, if I had been present? What wonderful events occurred?"

"I fought a duel with Mr. Stanson, and another with Dr. Leland."

"Now, Ella, tell me the whole story without any hyperbole."

The two girls, despite the ten years of difference in their ages, encircled each other's waists with their arms, and walked lovingly through the garden. Between them existed that peculiar kind of friendship which is sometimes developed under favorable influences. A fair young girl, a child, as it were, warmly attaches herself to one whose years exceed hers by a decade or more. She looks up to her elder friend with that beautiful, confiding spirit, which would be incompatible toward one of the same age. She seeks aid and advice from her more extensive experience. The elder is yet young, so that no want of sympathy is felt by the child. Nor is the conferring of benefits all on one side. The elder, possessing almost unbounded power over her more youthful friend, carefully leads her in the path which she has chosen for herself, and receives in return, not only a love as pure and fervent as any that she may hereafter enjoy, but also, a longer acquaintance with the thoughts and emotions exclusively belonging to the springtime of life, than she would have had if her connection had been wholly with those who had reached her own period of advancement.

As Adelaide looked down upon the sparkling but now saddened face which was upturned to hers, an indescribable emotion pervaded her breast, while she asked an explanation of what had evidently so wrought upon the frame of the impulsive girl.

With great candor, Ella detailed all the incidents of the previous evening, and then waited for Adelaide's comments.

"Did that conversation inflict upon you fearful dreams, give you the headache, and send you to me before five o'clock in the morning?"

"Even so; I became greatly excited."

"Now, Ella, dear, I must give you one caution. You have resolved to do all in your power for the promotion of good?"

"Yes, I hope to be very useful in some high station."

"You intend to do all that you can for the removal of the wrong which exists in the world, and for the development of the right. My dear child, the first lesson that you must learn is the fundamental principle of the Friends. You must acquire the power to control your passions. Unless you are cool and collected, you can not have perfect command of your resources. Without this command, it will be impossible for you to speak or write with due effect. You will forget half your arguments, check the flight of your imagination, and decidedly mar the beauty of that in which you appear to succeed. According to the account which you have given me, your efforts last evening were partially successful, but their consequences are most deplorable. You are quite ill. In fact, you became intoxicated last evening."

"Intoxicated!"

"Yes. What is the primary phenomenon attendant upon the drinking of ardent spirit? The brain is disordered by the liquor. Hence, the curious indications which betray the indulgence. A similar state of the brain may be induced without a single drop of fermented beverage. If the excitement were productive of any real good, we might find some apology for its gratification."

"But, can not we labor with more effect, when under the influence of excitement? Do we not need stimulus?"

"I grant that we do need stimulus, but I maintain that we should not procure it by any derangement of the system. If both body and mind are in a true normal state, they will act well without the aid of any other incentives, than those afforded by a good knowledge of the subject under discussion, and a thorough conviction of its importance. Devoid of these auxiliaries, a person may as well be silent. Why should Coleridge, with his genius, have sought the aid of opium! Why should Mrs. Radcliffe, with her exuberant fancy, have induced frightful dreams, by eating indigestible substances! They had mental power sufficient for the accomplishment of the tasks which they had assigned to themselves. The genuine orator can plead without the excitement produced by a glass of wine. You and I can labor in any department for which we are qualified, without inflaming our passions in order to attain to a certain measure of mental agitation. Intense cerebral excitement, by whatever means caused, is indisputably ruinous."

"Should not speakers and writers be in earnest?"

"Certainly, my dear Ella. Let them be, like the actor of whom we read the other day, 'terribly in earnest.' It is thus that they will achieve great exploits. But, let them beware of the least approach to any thing like delirium. They need the entire control of all their resources. Even Mrs. Hemans acknowledged that she could write better when her mind was calm and composed. Then it was that she had full dominion over her power of thought and fancy."

"But, should not you have been angry with Stanson?"

"No, nor should I have argued with him. Logic, upon that man, is equivalent to 'pearls before swine.' He is firmly imbedded in the dull flint of ignorance and stupidity. He did receive a common school education. With that as a basis, he might have raised a good superstructure. But his mind, never capacious, has been allowed to dwindle, without one addition to its original stock, so that it is now almost incapacitated for the reception of a new idea."

"Would you have sat quietly, and allowed him to talk in that style?"

Adelaide laughed. "I doubt whether I should, Ella, dear. But, instead of being angry, as you were, I should have been amused. In lieu of arguing, to convince him of his errors, I might have harangued, to show him that I could make statements which, to him, would be absolutely incontrovertible. Perfect self-control, however, would have characterized my demeanor. Most assuredly do I like an expressive countenance, and firmly do I believe that mine is of that description. But I wish also to obtain that power which was possessed by Pythagoras. We learn that he was so completely master of his face, that on it was never seen, joy, grief, or anger. I would *occasionally* use this power, not for *deception*, but for *concealment*—a distinction very wisely made by one of those sage Abbotts. It is sometimes very impolitic to let every thought be read by the beholder."

"But I should be sorry to look like a statue."

"So should I, at all times. But there are occasions when it is very undesirable to yield the key of our thoughts. Now, we will return to Stanson. It would be a fruitless task to attempt to convince him of any truth, unless it were advocated by the pastor. Let such people be engulfed in the whirlpool of their own insignificance. Besides, had you succeeded in your attempts to proselyte him, what good would have been effected? So contemptible an individual advocating woman's rights! I prefer that he should remain on the other side. The sentiments of a man like him are, comparatively speaking, nothing worth. He is a clog upon the movements of every party with which he chances to be connected. Shame it is that the vote of a man so ignorant and imbecile should have as much nominal value as that of the greatest statesman or scholar of the republic! Shame it is that such a man should be allowed the elective franchise; when a woman, even if her genius were equal to Shakspeare's, her learning to Sir William Jones', her political knowledge to Brougham's, or her diplomatic skill to Talleyrand's, would be sternly denied the privilege."

"Adelaide, Adelaide, now *you* are excited!" exclaimed Ella.

"*Earnest*, not excited, Ella," replied Adelaide, with a gay smile.

"Adelaide, you think that it is quite right for a woman to speak in public."

"Certainly. Every one who has the gift of eloquence, should receive an opportunity for its exercise. Dismiss all the tedious male speakers from their stations. Suffer only those to remain, who can instruct and entertain an audience. Substitute for the discharged bores, those women, whose talents, naturally good, have been improved by education. Society would then take an impetus, which would speed it onward and onward, till perfection were the result."

"If those are your opinions, why do you not enter our pulpit some day, and deliver an oration?"

"The perspective would be vastly pleasant, Ella! Before I should have finished my exordium, to be attacked by the four deacons, rushing upon me in a body, and then to be forcibly dragged from the house!"

Ella laughed, but Adelaide, although she faintly smiled, revealed upon her lofty countenance so keenly bitter an expression, that her young companion involuntarily retreated.

"If," resumed Adelaide, "a woman wishes to speak, she must, at present, beware of the pulpit, and choose a common lecture-room. Many have done this, and have shown, without dispute, that they could speak in public, and accomplish good, with no deserved reproach upon their delicacy. But I am not yet willing to make the attempt. I may do so in the course of a few years."

"What will Dr. Leland say?" asked Ella.

"I shall not consult him," answered Adelaide, with a haughty smile.

"Don't you like him?" inquired Ella, with all simplicity.

"I more than like him. I regard him as one of my best friends. Like every other educated person, of good natural endowments, and a proper degree of confidence, he is a very agreeable companion. I am indebted to him for much valuable instruction, and for many very pleasant hours of social intercourse. But I look upon no man as my oracle. His judgment is no better than mine. In a few years my mental acquirements will exceed his, both in extent and in value. I should not consult him on any topic of the kind, because I am already acquainted with his opinions, and with the fact that they are irrevocably formed. He is, too, a strict conservative, hating every kind of innovation. Again, he never argues with a woman. I doubt, indeed, whether he ever does with a man."

"Never argues with a woman!" repeated Ella, in a tone of surprise.

"Never. He dictates, and expects her to yield."

Ella thought of the previous evening, and smiled, as she remembered how magisterially he had announced his opinions, and checked the free utterance of hers.

"Dr. Leland, however," pursued Adelaide, "is more generous than a great many. He almost acknowledges that 'mind has no sex.' But he contends that the sphere of woman is exclusively private. He would have all the public business of life transacted by men, and would confine the women to a wretchedly contracted circle. He is proud of his wife's superior education, of her well-known colloquial power; but he will have all the happiness that she can confer restricted to himself, his children, and a small number of friends. Should she attempt to entertain an audience, I truly believe that he would sue for a divorce. This civilized refinement is only a whit nobler than the barbarian. He resembles many an Eastern sultan, who imprisons his wife in the seraglio, that none but himself may listen to the music of her voice, or behold the beauty of her countenance. The civilized husband monopolizes his wife's mind, and the demi-savage does her face.

"I think that I have discovered the true reason for all this. If women were allowed to exercise their talents in public, the men would often be defeated, and compelled to take quite an humble position. Do not Fanny Kemble's Shaksperian readings incomparably surpass those of any man? Is it not acknowledged that no young men are better qualified for college than those educated by our own Mrs. Ripley, of Concord? Did not Corinna so excel Pindar, in the poetic art, that she gained the prize five times? Who can compare with the learned Maria Gaetana Agnesi, in her ninth year delivering a Latin oration, and, in her eleventh, speaking Greek with fluency? Was she not, by reason of her skill in the languages, called a 'living polyglot?' Did she not also so excel in studies of another class, that, in her thirty-second year, she was appointed professor of mathematics, in the University of

Bologna? Did not the fame of Anna Maria Schur-
man extend over Europe, on account of her profi-
ciency in music, painting, sculpture, and engraving;
her knowledge of Greek, Hebrew, Syriac, Arabic,
and the modern languages? Was not the eloquence
of Mrs. Fry such that all ranks bowed before her
wondrous power? Does not Therese Robinson rank
well with our most learned men?

"Thus I might proceed to mention instance after
instance of female greatness, despite the obstruc-
tions interposed by men to deprive women of that
thorough education which they grant to youth of
their own sex. The truth is, dear Ella, women must
press forward, and demand that their educational
privileges shall be equal to those of the men. Now,
in consequence of the small share of favor yielded
to the prosecution of liberal studies, women must
acquire erudition by their own exertions. Like
Constantia Grierson, the celebrated Irish scholar
in Greek and Roman literature, they must be almost
entirely self-educated. Well, a better time is approaching. Meanwhile, let women do, as some of
both sexes have done, acquire, by their own efforts,
the learning which so enriches the mind."

"I will be a learned woman!" exclaimed Ella.
" I will study with all my might!"

" Then, my dear, you must be careful to avoid
every species of intoxication. Be very temperate.
If you lose your health, although you may live many
years, you will be obliged to study with great mod-

eration, and will be prevented from ever making any remarkable attainments."

"I now feel quite well," answered Ella, merrily bounding forward. "I am sure that I can study." Suddenly changing her tone, she cried, "Alas! it is my day for music. I never shall excel in that branch. I wish that papa would allow me to abandon the piano. How much time I should have for other studies! Adelaide, why have you never learned music?"

"In my early youth, I should have replied that I could not afford the expense. Now, I prefer to spend what time I have for study upon subjects for which I have greater talent. Besides, music, however beautiful, is not so congenial to my taste, as conversation with those who have depth of thought, and ability of expression. Many young ladies and gentlemen of the present age are good pianists, but how few have that power to which Wilkes alluded, when he said that he could, at any time, 'talk away his ugly face in five minutes.'"

"I would rather listen to your conversation than to Delia's singing and playing," observed Ella.

"Delia ought to sing and play much more than she is in the habit of doing, but I doubt whether it is your duty or mine ever to make the attempt. She has decided musical talent. Were it properly cultivated, she might, in a few years, gain distinction, equal, perhaps, to that of 'the sweet singer from Sweden.'"

"Oh, how I wish that I could hear Jenny Lind! If Delia should become a good musician, ought she to sing in public?"

"Answer your own question, Ella. Would it be right to restrict the enjoyment of so much pure happiness to a few individuals? If I could sing like Jenny Lind, I would go through the world, charming people with my voice. If I could read like Fanny Kemble, I would also employ my power for the benefit of the human race. While entranced by her performances, I yet retained sufficient self-possession, not only to notice the effect upon my own mind, but also upon that of the other auditors. In truth, Ella, I should prefer her sphere to Jenny's. I rank such reading as hers far higher than any singing which the world can produce. Ah! here is Rose, calling me to breakfast. Stay with us this morning, dear Ella."

While Ella was deliberating whether she could thus indulge herself, Dora's pretty face appeared over the garden gate, and her melodious, Hibernian voice was heard, "Sure, Miss Ella, I've been a looking for you this half hour. Your ma says you must come home."

"Must, must," repeated Ella, with a sigh. "*Must* is the most hateful word in the English language. It is fit to be pronounced only by the 'skinny lips' of Macbeth's witches, and not by yours of beautiful carnation, Dora. Good-bye, Adelaide. Oh, wait a moment, I *must* tell you something."

"Not now, my love, your mother has sent for you."

"Nay, but you *must* hear me. Dr. Leland said—"

"You have told me all that he said."

"All that he said last evening, but, this is something which I heard from another person. It closely concerns yourself."

"What is it?" asked Adelaide, without any manifestation of curiosity.

"That he intended soon to find time to call and remind you of certain verses in the writings of St. Paul."

"Oh," replied Adelaide, gravely, "if his time is very much occupied, he need not subject himself to any inconvenience on my account. I am very well acquainted with the 'Apostle to the Gentiles.' I frequently converse with him."

"Come, come, Miss Ella," called Dora, with a little of her lady's impatience.

"Adieu, dear Adelaide," said Ella, running to overtake the domestic, whose feet were in the direction of Mr. Thornton's, but whose face was almost fronting Captain Wilmot's, to the great danger of dislocating her neck.

XV.

MESMERISM.

'All things being are in mystery; we expound mysteries by mysteries;
And yet the secret of them all is one in simple grandeur:
All intricate, yet each path plain, to those who know the way;
All unapproachable, yet easy of access, to them that hold the key."

MARTIN F. TUPPER.

WHEN Ella entered the parlor, she found the family too deeply engrossed by conversation to notice her arrival. She glided toward her brother Charles, around whom the others appeared to be gathered, and saw that the commotion had been excited by some announcement in the newspaper.

"Ella dear," said Charles, "listen to this curious advertisement:

"'William Norwood, professor of the sublime science of the immortal Mesmer, here proclaims, that on Thursday evening, he will endeavor to illumine the minds of the inhabitants of Clinton, by disseminating through Albion Hall rays of that magnificent sun which has dawned upon himself; in other words, he will give an elucidation of that newly-discovered remedy for the evils which afflict mankind. By means of his art, he will compel his subject to direct his mental vision into the system of a person diseased, whether by acute or chronic maladies, will immediately discover the true nature of the disorder, and will satisfactorily prescribe remedies for a thorough cure.

"'He will gladly gratify the curiosity of any persons who desire to receive intelligence of absent friends, by revealing an exact account of their situation, their health, and the occupation in which they may be engaged.

" ' Those who object to a personal examination for disease, may send a lock of their hair. With this simple substitute, the professor, by means of his great skill, can obtain the same results. The compensation demanded will, of course, be greater, than as if the examination were more directly made, but in no case will the charge be exorbitant.' "

"What a specimen of grandiloquence!" exclaimed Ella, laughing merrily; "the man's character must be a singular combination of assumption and pomposity."

"Well, leaving the style, what do you think of the substance?"

"His pretensions are as comic as they are preposterous. Does he mean that he can invisibly enter a room in Boston or New Orleans, and tell us how the inmates are employed?"

"Even so."

"That he can look within the frame of a sick person, and learn the nature of the malady?"

"The same."

"The reality of the Salem Witchcraft would be quite as credible."

"Even that absurdity received full credence from Cotton Mather," replied Charles, with great gravity.

"Cotton Mather was a learned man and a Christian," remarked Mr. Thornton, as if he thought himself called upon to defend a calumniated saint.

"And a good minister," chimed in Mrs. Thornton.

"But, would you vindicate the belief in witchcraft?" asked Charles, with a quiet smile, "because Cotton Mather was among its supporters?"

"No, my son," answered Mr. Thornton, "but my thoughts were wandering amid that strange delusion; and I was pained, as I frequently am, by a glance at the ridicule which the good men of those days now so often receive."

"Good men," repeated Ella, "to press one to death, and to hang others, both men and women, merely because the poor wretches were accused by some silly children!"

"I fancy, Ella," retorted her mother, "that if you had lived at that time, you would have joined those silly children. You are very fond of doing any thing to attract attention."

"I, mamma," said poor Ella, crimsoning at the unkind imputation.

"Yes, you, Miss Ella."

"Am I bold, papa?" appealed Ella, springing upon her father's knee, with as much ease as little Carrie would have shown, "am I conceited?"

"Why," hesitated Mr. Thornton, kissing the fair brow of his daughter, "you are not a true violet, but, in my opinion, you are quite as agreeable as if you were. But, hear now what I have to say with regard to some of the reprehensible conduct of our ancestors. Independent as they professed to be in matters of judgment, they were still greatly influenced by the views maintained in the mother country. England was yet under the dominion of superstition. Even the renowned Sir Matthew Hale tried and condemned a great many who were charged with the supposed crime of witchcraft."

"Ella," said Charles, "Cotton Mather wrote that little book which you were reading the other day; 'Essays on Doing Good.' Do you know that Dr. Franklin attributed all his usefulness to a perusal of that volume?"

"Dr. Franklin is no favorite of mine. People would be very mean, if they were to observe all the maxims inculcated in his 'Poor Richard.'"

Mr. Thornton, who always considered an attack upon Franklin or Washington as an act of sacrilege, hastened to recall attention to the main subject, by saying, "Who will go to the lecture this evening?"

"Not I, sir," answered Charles; "I feel quite sure that this Norwood, whether or not he has any claim to the title of *professor*, is an ignorant pretender."

"Where is your proof?"

"Look at his advertisement. To say nothing of that ridiculous first sentence, here is a statement which positively attests his ignorance. 'Newly-discovered remedy!' One would infer that animal magnetism had been known only within a few years, whereas, Mesmer, its founder, proclaimed the doctrine in 1766. I doubt whether Professor Norwood merits the least attention. I shall not waste my evening upon him."

"Oh, men differ as to the meaning of words referring to time," returned Mr. Thornton, with great deliberation; "I advise you to go, Charles."

"I have another reason for not attending, sir. Rose is going to a party. Of course, Captain Wilmot's daughters never leave him without a companion. Adelaide will remain at home this evening. Consequently, my time will be occupied in reading or conversing with her."

"Certainly, my son. Ella, should you like to go with me?"

"Yes, indeed, papa. I am curious to know whether the lecturer will mention Miss Martineau and her mad cow."

"I should be glad of some information concerning that cow's health," observed Charles, laughing. "If Miss Martineau succeeds in her efforts to accomplish a cure, I hope that she will employ her skill in Mesmerism to relieve her own defective hearing."

"Have you any confidence in Mesmerism?"

"Yes, I believe that it is one of many remedial agents; but, so full of mystery is the subject, that I would not trust an unprofessional person with its administration. I could rely only upon an experienced physician."

That evening, Mr. and Mrs. Thornton, accompanied by Delia and Ella, proceeded to the room mentioned in the advertisement. In truth, Mr. Thornton had some hope that Mesmerism might relieve Delia of her indescribable malady.

Albion Hall, which had probably thus been named by some wag, from the abundance of white-wash bestowed upon its adornment, was early filled by the lovers of the marvelous.

The next day, when the four attempted to give Charles some account of the lecture, they appeared very much as if their minds had indeed been sent on some distant excursion by the boastful professor. Even Ella's usually retentive memory could not furnish a good abstract of the evening's entertainment.

"For my part," confessed Mr. Thornton, as he paused in despair, "I must say, that the young man glanced at so many subjects, and gave such a profusion of anecdotes, that my brain has blended them all together in dire confusion."

"That is frequently the case," observed Charles; "do you not remember Basil Hall's singular comments after spending an evening with Sir Walter Scott? The distinguished novelist related so many stories, that the unfortunate Basil had hardly a distinct recollection of any one of the number."

"Well," declared Mrs. Thornton, "I never heard so many falsehoods told in one lecture."

"My dear," remonstrated her husband, "as we are entirely ignorant of medicine, we can not judge whether or not the young man were telling the truth."

"If all those absurdities were true, I am ready to believe in witchcraft."

"Oh, mamma," entreated Charles, with mock horror, "do not reach that point. Delia, have you entirely forgotten the lecture?"

"I was so terrified," answered the young lady, "that I could not duly attend to the lecture. His experiments upon that poor boy, whom he called his subject, were frightful. By his maneuvers, he caused him to fall asleep, and then questioned him upon different topics. I would not be thus served."

"Not even with the hope of a cure?"

"Not if Norwood were the operator."

"You are right, sister. Only a physician should practice Mesmerism. I feel certain that Norwood has studied neither physiology nor pathology."

"He told us that Mesmer was a physician," said Ella, brightening with the recollection.

"Very good. No one will dispute that statement. Come, Ella, try to recall some other facts."

"He said that Mesmer began to practice with magnetized rods, which he had obtained from a Jesuit."

"What was the Jesuit's name?"

"He did not say."

"It was Holl. I have read an account of the affair. Proceed, Ella."

"Mesmer soon discovered that his hands could be

as effectual as the rods. His success was so remarkable, that he acquired renown, made many proselytes, and founded a school. A large majority of his
pupils became celebrated."

"I remember," exclaimed Delia, with a sudden
effort, "what was said of king Clovis. The monarch dreamed that he could cure a certain scrofulous
man by touching his neck. His dream was verified.
Afterward, the power of removing scrofula by touching remained a prerogative of the royal family in
France."

"Delia," inquired Charles, abruptly, "did this
Norwood, with whom I have no patience, assert that
diseases were actually cured by the touch of those
royal Frenchmen?"

"He appeared to have entire confidence in the
doctrine. He told us also that the same mode was
soon practiced by other sovereigns. James the
Second, after his exile from England, was engaged
in some of the French hospitals, as a toucher for
scrofula."

Charles gazed intently upon the ceiling, magnan-
imously attempting to repress his inclination to
laugh.

"I presume that he also detailed the process of
touching, as reported by Cavalli, the Venetian
embassador, in the time of Francis?"

All asserted that no such name had been mentioned.

"Ah, I believe that, with my limited knowledge

of Mesmerism, I could give a better lecture than
you heard last evening—"

"Charles," interrupted his mother, "you are as
conceited as Ella."

"Oh, mamma," replied the young gentleman,
with an assumption of the sententious, "a just ap-
preciation of one's individual merit should not
receive the misnomer of self-conceit. I would em-
bellish my lecture with sundry very fine stories of
which Norwood has never heard. How full of
pathos would be my description of Edward the
Confessor, the first English king who touched for
scrofula! How well would I enlarge upon the enthusiastic description of Cavalli, given in the reign
of the French king, Francis! He tells us that the
ceremony was performed on the day of some holy
festival. Before touching, the king confessed, and
received the sacrament. These preliminaries ended,
he made the sign of the cross upon the patient,
saying, 'The king touches, may God cure thee.'
How romantic the scene! See what an effect may
be produced by imagination! The spectacle must
have been truly imposing in the eyes of the ignorant
multitude."

"Then you do not believe that Francis, or any
other king, ever possessed this power?"

"No, Ella, I am a very skeptic as far as the marvelous is concerned. The days of miracles long
since ceased. The belief in the efficacy of the royal touch must be numbered with the superstitions

of by-gone days. Do you not know that Johnson, the eminent lexicographer, was taken, during his scrofulous childhood, to Queen Anne, with the vain hope of a cure. But the hand of the royal lady had no sanative power. If the lecturer knew of this fact, he was not sufficiently candid to communicate it to his hearers. But could not you decide whether Norwood related those stories as if he believed them, or merely as curious instances of the effect of superstition, aided by imagination?"

" He seemed to give them entire credence, and to explain them by the principles of Mesmerism."

" What other topics were discussed?"

"So many that I can not remember them. He spoke of health, disease, and dying; of Gassner, Cochran, and Swedenborg."

"I perceive that he lectured without much method. Now, tell me of the Mesmeric sleep."

" He induced sleep in his own subject by a simple wave of the hand. This, he said, was attributed to the power which he had acquired over the lad."

"I pity that youth. How can his parents allow him to be the victim of such a man! If there is any truth in Mesmerism, his system must be injured by so frequent an endurance of that unnatural sleep."

" After those experiments, he boldly challenged any of the auditors to approach, that he might show, by his success with them, that no collusion existed between himself and his own subject."

" Was the summons answered?"

"At first, no one moved. The lecturer then observed, that, if he chose, he could will them to approach, but he should prefer volunteers. Finally, two boys crept timidly upon the platform."

"Who were they?"

"Frank Lewis and Arthur Hoyt. The lecturer said that he should have time only for one."

"I can tell which was chosen: Arthur."

"Right, but are you really a conjurer, Charles?"

"Those who know more of a subject than others are the true conjurers, Ella. Arthur was selected on account of his red hair and transparent complexion. His organization well qualifies him for a Mesmeric subject. Norwood must have succeeded."

"Unfortunately, the nine o'clock bell rang. The lecturer, with the appearance of deep regret, said that he was well aware of the good habits observed by the Clintonians, and that he would not therefore detain them any longer. The time had come for the close of the performance."

Charles gave a prolonged "*Ah!*" and began to pace the room, apparently struggling with his thoughts.

"As we were leaving the hall," resumed Ella, the lecturer reminded us of his advertisement, and said that he might be consulted at his boarding-house, by any who desired the benefit of his skill."

At that moment, Mrs. Stipend's little daughter was ushered into the room. Her mother had sent her with the message, that Professor Norwood was about to magnetize a lady who had long been ill with rheumatism; and, that having heard of Miss Thornton's indisposition, he should be happy to allow her family to witness the operation, hoping that they would not object to intrust him with the treatment of her case.

"Let us go, by all means," proposed Mr. Thornton.

"Sir," entreated Charles, "do not, I implore you."

"Why, Charles, you have yourself expressed some belief in Mesmerism."

"Yes, sir, I confidently believe that it is a curative agent; but, also, that it is a subject requiring profound medical knowledge for its safe application. No ignorant person should be intrusted with its management."

"My son, you are very positive in your condemnation of this lecturer."

Charles hesitated a moment, and then quietly observed, "For a few months he was my roommate at college. He gained distinction in no one branch. From pure benevolence, I attempted to act in the capacity of private tutor. I hope never again to be favored with such a pupil. Ludicrous as was the advertisement in yesterday's paper, it was probably written by some scrivener, possessing a little more knowledge than himself. At the end of the first term, he was expelled from college for incompetency, or, in the more polite phrase ology of the West-Pointers, 'his resignation was accepted.'"

Mr. Thornton received this communication with a blank visage. In plain truth, his curiosity had been excited to behold the experiments. As he prepared for the expedition, he defended himself by saying, "But, Charles, some men who made no figure at college, have since become celebrated."

"Yes, sir, but those were not stupid men. They were merely indolent. They redeemed their time and their reputation as well as they could by subsequent study. No man, naturally dull, ever became noted, except for folly. Lord Timothy Dexter's fame was quite unenviable."

For once Mr. Thornton was obstinate. He deliberately drew on his gloves.

"Delia," said Charles, as the young girl rose to accompany her father, "do not submit to any of the *professor's* experiments."

"I assure you, Charles, I do not intend even to make known my illness. I am going, like papa, from motives of curiosity."

Ella, too, like the Athenians of old, eager "to tell, or to hear some new thing," hastily arrayed herself for a walk to Mrs. Stipend's. As she was leaving the room, she pleasantly said to her brother, "You chose a very appropriate profession. You were born for a schoolmaster. My knowledge of the lecture was most chaotic, till you drew it from me by your cross-questioning."

"Observe closely what you see at Mrs. Stipend's, for I shall depend upon you for an account."

An hour afterward, Ella bounded into the room, exclaiming, "All is at an end. Norwood has failed. After a deal of preparation, he took Mrs. Gorham's hands in his, and looked into her eyes, till I thought that her face would ever after retain the carnation hue which it had suddenly assumed. Then he waved his long arms, and performed so many manipulations, that I think of sketching them from memory for the next edition of the Comic Almanac. But Mrs. Gorham sat with her eyes wide open, and manifested not the least inclination to sleep. The professor was evidently vexed. He declared that she was a person entirely devoid of impressibility."

"Did Norwood acknowledge his defeat?"

"Oh, no. He boldly asserted that Mrs. Gorham was one of the very few whom Mesmerism could not benefit."

"What followed?"

"The professor whispered to Mrs. Stipend, who immediately led him to papa, and performed the ceremony of introduction. He asked permission to magnetize Delia. Papa replied, that if Delia were willing, he might do so at our house, with no witness but mamma. Norwood then bowed to my sister, and waited for her to speak. She answered that she would, on no account, submit to the process."

"Delia is a rational girl," observed Charles, with a sigh of relief.

"Now, brother, what do you think of the professor and his science?"

"My opinion remains unchanged. I believe, that in some disorders, Mesmerism may be employed with benefit to the patient; but, that so mysterious an agent should never be trusted in the hands of those who have not received a thorough medical education. Norwood must be ranked in the company of itinerant lecturers, who, without regular study or education, have acquired a superficial knowledge of some subject, and who endeavor to make a fortune, as perambulatory teachers. Solitary study, Ella, is the best method of gaining instruction."

"Do you despise lectures?"

"By no means. I have a very high opinion of oral instruction, when it is imparted by those who are truly competent. But I prefer books. The silent teachers are the best."

XVI.

LES VOILÀ.

"A man in many a country town, we know,
Professes openly with death to wrestle;
Entering the field against the grimly foe,
Armed with a mortar and a pestle."—COLMAN, *the Younger*

To give a full detail of all the physicians, real or pretended, who visited that devoted town of Clinton, during the next few weeks, would require more space than I am disposed to allow. I will briefly mention a few of the most prominent.

First in order came a disciple of the renowned Dr. Graham, who gave a formidable course of lectures, and established himself in the village, with the hope of obtaining proselytes. He was truly a man of one idea, *dietetics*. He began his first lecture with the ominous quotation, "We dig our graves with our teeth." He then proceeded to demonstrate that all the evils to which human beings are liable, result either from intemperance in eating, or from the use of improper articles of food. The Clintonians, with the exception of the grocers, were so reasonable as to nod assent, when he affirmed that the gout was caused chiefly by wine and brandy; but, when his censures were leveled at certain delicious edibles, which had always been considered perfectly harmless, all who regarded eating even as a minor pleasure, shook their heads, and loyally returned to the doctrines by which they had previously been guided. When mince pie, that pride of the housewife, who never thinks that too many ingredients can be blended in this most complex and mysterious of dainties, was denounced as prime agent in the cause of disease, every matron whispered to her next neighbor, that the man was evidently unendowed with the most prevalent of Nature's gifts, plain common-sense. When he condemned the practice of fattening fowls for New England's great, but most matter-of-fact festival, Thanksgiving, as worthy only of the degraded epicures of ancient Sybaris, every farmer who had honored Albion Hall with his presence, was ready to aim, at least, a pitchfork, at the head of the gaunt figure so eloquently declaiming against usages which had existed from what they considered "time immemorial." When he denounced spice and pepper as substances having a direct tendency to shorten life, several aged ladies and gentlemen, who had eaten food prepared with condiments from their infancy, shrugged their venerable shoulders in utter disdain at what they regarded the lecturer's ignorance. When he inveighed against the various forms of candy and comfit, the children's lips quivered for one moment, but danced in merry smiles the next, as they saw the stern visage of their staunch friend the confectioner, who, if any truth may be found in physiognomy, looked ready to challenge the Grahamite to mortal combat. When, moreover, the haggard orator, for, in personal appearance he was a living skeleton, remonstrated with his auditors concerning the quantity of food generally taken, affirming, with great solemnity, that they eat far more than was requisite for the sustenance of life, several apoplectic veterans boldly declared that they would rather die of repletion than of inanition. When he loudly fulminated against the use of salt, so commonly demanded to render food palatable, and averred that this practice, universal as it had become, was of a highly destructive nature, every individual in the hall began to regard the speaker as a promising candidate for the retreat at Worcester. When, also, he asserted that meat, if eaten at all, would be far less detrimental to the health, if, instead of being allowed to come in contact with fire, it were served up in its crude state, every hearer viewed him as one who had actually escaped from said retreat, and who was no longer to be trusted among people yet retaining possession of their sanity.

This Grahamite was not, however, one of the most rigid graduates of his school. Although he prudently paused before reaching its most extravagant rules, he went quite too far for the inhabitants of Clinton, the majority of whom were accustomed cordially to sympathize with the royal bard, when he gratefully exclaimed, "Who satisfieth thy mouth with good things, so that thy youth is renewed like the eagle's."

Before the Clintonians had recovered from the effects of the Grahamite's strictures, they were thrown into consternation by the necessity of listening to the doctrines promulgated by a lecturer of quite a different order. He styled himself a Thomsonian physician. Steam was his ruling idea. Only one lecture was given by this claimant for popular favor. The exordium was a bold declaration that the life of every one was in peril, until the same medical system was held which he was about to explain that evening. The people raised their eyes in astonishment, and wondered that they had already lived so long. With due heed did they listen to the arguments of the advocate of Steam. Although not highly educated, he was intelligent and entertaining, so that he commanded the attention of all. He expatiated upon the good which had been effected by the application of the vapor bath, and by the swallowing of cayenne and other scorching medicines. This part was very terrible to the lovers of Nature's pure beverage, sparkling fresh from the hill-side. The peroration consisted of a heart-stirring appeal to the Clintonians, to avail themselves of his excellent apparatus for the administration of vapor baths.

Whatever benefit some classes of patients might have derived from his system, if moderately pursued, the extravagance of this lecturer defeated his object. All the invalids of the place preferred ice cream and strawberries to Cayenne and hot drops; and the refreshing cold bath to the enervating vapor. He soon left the place, taking with him his whole stock of Heclaian medicines, and his excellent Vesuvian apparatus.

Next came a most extraordinary pretender. His claims to notice were not founded upon any educational advantages. He had not walked the hospitals of Europe, in quest of thorough, practical knowledge. He could not even exhibit a diploma granted by any American institution. The garb in which his thoughts were clothed did, indeed, betray that he had received no education worthy of the name. But he made not the slightest attempt to conceal his ignorance. He actually boasted that he was indebted to neither books nor lectures for his art. He had a patent which, he averred, no one could dispute. Nature had singled him from among men as a healer of disease. On him, had she bestowed a glorious distinction, of which any learned doctor would have been proud. Not one of England's titled sons had received a nobler heritage. Greater were his heraldic honors than those belonging to the sons of the peerage. He was—the seventh son of a seventh son. As such, who could dispute his right to practice without overcoming one of those obstacles which are placed in the way of students not thus royally descended!

But his claims were advanced very near the middle of the nineteenth century. Even then were people discussing the question concerning the true center of the great circle. The subject had been introduced at every fireside. In the highly cultivated town of Clinton, the seventh son of a seventh son should not have expected to receive much attention. Mr. Stanson did, however, request him to come and prescribe for his wife, whose symptoms were daily becoming more and more alarming. But, when the anxious husband, accompanied by the inheritor of medical power, entered by the front door, the patient, with fearful majesty of mien, vanished through the opposite portal, taking with her "Milton on Divorce."

After the lapse of one week, during which, the new-comer was consulted by no other person, he sadly departed in the way that he had come, a simple pedestrian, with his wardrobe inclosed in a blue and yellow cotton handkerchief.

I say nothing of a very entertaining type doctor with his curious symbols. I pause not to dilate upon the merits of a mysterious Indian seer. I disdain to call your attention to a noted empiric, with his one remedy for every kind of disease.

I here dismiss the worshipful company of physicians, by whom the devoted town of Clinton was awhile infested. Early in the autumn, the field was again clear. All had disappeared, save the long-established resident. Dr. Perry again walked proudly through the streets of the village, and rode cheerily over the hills to the more distant farms. His apothecary, also, who, during the whole summer, had been in a woful state of nervous agitation, so that he could hardly distinguish between senna, calomel, and sanguinaria, now joyously deciphered recipes, and merrily plied his pestle and mortar.

XVII.

LAW.

"If thou well observe
The rule of *Not too much*; by temperance taught,
In what thou eat'st and drink'st; seeking from thence
Due nourishment, not gluttonous delight,
Till many years over thy head return:
So mayst thou live; till, like ripe fruit, thou drop
Into thy mother's lap; or be with ease
Gather'd, not harshly pluck'd; for death mature."—MILTON.

WAS there, then, no cure for Delia? Would she submit to no physician? Would none offer the right prescription? Was there no drug in the whole pharmacopœia which might effect a favorable change in her symptoms? Or, was it true, that no medicine was needed, that relief must be sought in some other way?

One pleasant autumn day, Delia expressed a wish to visit Adelaide. Charles gladly drove her to Captain Wilmot's, in a low, easy chaise, and promised to come for her early in the evening.

During several hours, the young invalid amused herself with listening to the captain's nautical stories, and with the general conversation of the family. In the afternoon, while the sun was yet high, and the earth warm, Adelaide invited her guest to accompany her in a short ramble through the neighboring forest. Delia languidly assented, and, leaning upon the arm of her more robust friend, slowly traversed the road leading to Adelaide's favorite retreat. Her former prejudices against the lady of her brother's choice had long since vanished. Admiration for Adelaide's heroic character had been the germ. This had gradually developed into fervent love. They advanced leisurely, Delia pausing every few moments, and asserting that she could not walk as rapidly as one who had never known ill health. Adelaide carefully checked her own eager footsteps. The trees were now beginning to assume their gorgeous, autumnal hues. The green shades, in their varied beauty, were yet seen, but, occasionally, a branch, decked with bright, golden leaves, met the eye of the beholder. Then, the brilliant scarlet declared that its turn had come. Anon, the deep, rich purple blushed in the vale. Dappled leaves of surpassing beauty strewed the ground.

"Look, look, Delia!" exclaimed Adelaide, with rapture, as a specimen of uncommon magnificence fluttered in the air.

Delia wearily turned her head, and then sadly rested her glance upon the trees, eloquent in their prophetic beauty. A few tears fell from her eyes. Adelaide did not notice the weakness, but said, with animation, "Has not this well been called 'The coronation of the year?' How exquisite is the scene!"

"Grand as is the view," replied Delia, "it never affords me any pleasure. I think of the dread winter which must so soon follow. I feel fatigued as I anticipate the long months of bitter cold. To me, this season gives nothing to which I can apply the epithet *regal*. Do not speak of a coronation."

"Let us then view the subject in a different light. Another idea, quite as beautiful, but more tranquil, has been suggested. A certain anonymous writer has, with deep feeling, and the genuine spirit of poetry, styled Autumn, 'The Sabbath of the year.' Do you not remember the lines,

> "'And then the wind ariseth slow,
>   And giveth out a psalm,
> And the organ-pipes begin to blow,
>   Within the forest calm:
> Then all the trees lift up their hands,
>   And lift their voices higher,
> And sing the notes of spirit-bands,
>   In full and glorious choir.

> "'Yes! 'tis the Sabbath of the year,
>   And it doth surely seem—
> (But words of reverence and of fear
>   Should speak of such a theme),
> That the corn is gather'd for the bread,
>   And the berries for the wine,
> And a sacramental feast is spread,
>   Like the Christian's pardon-sign.

"How truthful are these stanzas! I can even fancy the author standing in this forest, and calmly, but joyously surveying the scene."

Delia was well-nigh faint on beholding the excess of health and spirits with which Adelaide was overflowing. Such a contrast to her own mournful state! She threw herself upon the prostrate trunk of an aged oak. Adelaide sat down by her side, casting only one wistful glance into the depths of the forest.

"Adelaide," said Delia, with a trembling voice, "had you quoted the sermon instead of the anthem, you would have more accurately expressed my feelings. I can better respond to the second stanza.

> "'With a deep, earnest voice he saith,
>   And yet a voice of grief,
> Fitting the minister of Death,
>   So fade all as a leaf;
> And your iniquities, like the wind,
>   Have taken ye away!
> So, fading flutterers, weak and blind,
>   Repent, return, and pray.'

"Oh, Adelaide, I must die. I am doomed, in my youth, to. lie down in the dark grave. I can not meet death like the saint or the hero. I have too much faith in eternity to comprehend the tranquillity with which Hume jested of Charon. I have too little to exclaim with the apostle, 'Oh, Death, where is thy sting!' But the decree has gone forth. I must die."

"To what false prophet have you been listening?" asked Adelaide, endeavoring to infuse a yet higher degree of cheerfulness into her tones.

"To more than one true prophet. Look at my pale face, my hollow eyes. Feel the irregular beating of my pulse. Listen to the throbbing of my heart, which proclaims but too plainly that its movements are not those of health. I can not live. I am not willing to die."

Adelaide mused a moment, as if studying the best course to pursue. At length, she deliberately said, "I should not be willing to die."

Delia raised her eyes in astonishment.

"You expect that heaven will be your home after death!"

"I hope that it will," replied Adelaide, with great seriousness of manner.

"Then, why should you regret leaving earth?"

"I will tell you. Unnumbered years will be spent in heaven. Every moment will afford happiness. This life, beautiful as it is, can not be compared with that. But, were I immediately transported to the celestial world, my happiness would be less intense, than if I were to remain on earth till the period of old age. I have now reached maturity. I am beginning to have the full exercise of all my powers. If I live fifty years longer, I can accomplish a vast deal of good, the remembrance of which will be a source of happiness even in heaven. What can not be done in fifty years, by one who is determined to employ all her time and influence for the promotion of the true and the right!"

Delia's thoughts, thus suddenly turned into this

new channel, were entirely diverted from her own health.

"Fifty years!" she exclaimed, "what a space of time! A whole half-century! How many changes will occur! I should like to see the end of that period. I am five years younger than you. If I had a good constitution, I might hope to live."

Here, Delia looked sorrowfully upon her transparent hands.

"To think," resumed Adelaide, "of the great number of days in all those years; that on every one of those days, we may both receive and impart happiness! Daily and hourly may we gain new ideas. Does it not seem, Delia, as if life were indeed a noble boon? Might we not, at the end of that time, be truly glorious beings?"

Delia sighed. Life was beginning to appear desirable, not merely from the dread of death, but from the objects which might be attained, the felicity which might be enjoyed.

"Oh, that I were well!" she bitterly exclaimed. "Oh, that I could hear of some eminent physician, who might cure my disease!"

Adelaide mentally rejoiced. She now saw that she could proceed with safety.

"Delia," she asked, "why so much confidence in physicians? One of the most distinguished of their number, James Johnson, of Great Britain, frankly acknowledges that the art practiced by his profession is conjectural, and honestly confesses that the

world would do quite as well without medical
aid."

"Do you agree with him?"

"Not to the full extent. His remark was occasioned by a contemplation of the evils which result
from exclusive dependence upon the skill of the
physician. He directly implies that people disregard the laws of life and health, thinking that they
can trust to men of his profession, for relief from
the disorders which they have brought upon themselves. But I greatly honor physicians. Their
services would seldom be needed if the laws of
physiology were obeyed. To whom, however, are
we indebted for a knowledge of those laws? To
those physicians who have studied Nature, and
revealed her mysteries. But, when we look abroad
over the community, we can not fail to see that the
incurable are rarely relieved by medicine, and that
the curable would generally be much better without
its use. I am not surprised that Grace Aguilar was
always suffering, nor that she died at the early age
of thirty-one. We read that from the age of three
years, she was almost constantly under the care of a
physician."

"If you were ill," inquired Delia, "would you
not consult a physician?"

"Disease would be so at variance with my constitution," replied Adelaide, smiling, "that I can
hardly answer that question. If I should be attacked by any acute malady, such as fever or cho-

lera, I should certainly desire the attendance of one who had made sickness and its remedy his study, that the foe might speedily be expelled from my system. In a chronic complaint, very little can be effected by medical art. If the patient is ignorant, some judicious advice may be given by his physician. But a cure, if it come at all, will be far distant; and if death must be the termination, not much can be done by drugs to arrest its progress."

Delia shuddered. "Tell me, Adelaide, what will be my fate. Must I die?"

The lips of the young girl quivered as she looked anxiously into the countenance of her friend. Adelaide hastily soothed her.

"Be calm, my dear, while I tell you that restoration to health depends upon your own exertions."

"Only show me how I can be well. I so long for life and health."

"Listen carefully to one explanation. If any organ were radically diseased, no hope of cure could be entertained. But I have reason to believe that your brain, heart, lungs, etc., are in good order."

"I am not sure, Adelaide," answered the invalid, with tremulous accents; "I have a great deal of the headache. My heart often beats with great violence. Occasionally, I have hectic flushes."

"Those symptoms indicate that you are far from well, but they do not positively prove that you are fatally diseased. If you have carefully observed your own ailments, you must remember that every headache was caused by some indiscretion which might have been avoided. Yours is not a very dangerous pain. It may become such, if not judiciously managed. Can you mention one headache, which was not produced by too great indulgence of appetite, by prolonged reading, by exposure to a sun hotter than your constitution could bear, or by remaining in an imperfectly ventilated apartment?"

"Are those the causes of pain in the head?"

"Of such pain as troubles you. Banish the cause, and you will escape the effect."

"But my stomach must be injured by over-eating. Why should my head suffer?"

"Because of the connection which exists between the head and the stomach. The pain in the head is sympathetic. Thus it is also with palpitation of the heart. That symptom does, in some cases, evince a diseased state of this grand muscle. But very often, it simply declares, that the heart is sympathizing with some other organ. Nervous and dyspeptic patients frequently suffer from palpitation. Hectic fever is also an attendant of several complaints. But this symptom, although in some states alarming, in others merely shows that the health needs attention in order to prevent any thing of a more serious tendency. Such indications are beacon-lights, warning us of the evil which will ensue if heed is not given to the signals."

For a few moments, Delia was absorbed in

thought. She broke silence by saying, "Then a physician would be of no service to me."

"Unless he had the condescension to give you a few lessons in physiology, and to insist upon their practical application. But a physician's province is to cure actual disease. He usually finds so much of this, that he will not pause to enlighten those who might be saved by a little instruction. Call in almost any of the faculty. He would feel as if he were summoned for the purpose of prescribing some drug. This would be injurious rather than beneficial."

"Do you despise all the remedies which have been discovered with so much exertion?"

"By no means. I agree with the Son of Sirach: 'The Lord hath created medicines out of the earth; and he that is wise will not abhor them.' It is only the abuse which I condemn. Very little is ever needed. People often make themselves ill by the practice of swallowing medicinal substances."

"But how can I obtain relief if I take nothing to remove my pain and weakness?"

"Did you ever read the anecdote of the purchaser of sanative wisdom? Notice was given that a late distinguished physician had left a book containing the secret of health. Eager to secure the prize, an invalid felt no hesitation in paying quite a large sum for the valuable manuscript. To his astonishment, he found that the revelation, to which he had looked with so much confidence, consisted of only four simple maxims: 'Rise early; keep the back straight; the head cool; the feet warm.' It is not surprising that he was somewhat exasperated. Resolving, however, not to be a loser by his extravagant purchase, he commenced a course of strict conformity to the four rules. In consequence, his health improved to an extent which he had doubtless believed impossible."

"Do you regard that as a true story?" asked Delia, with an earnestness which she seldom manifested.

"I see no reason to doubt its authenticity. It is, at least, probable."

"If I were to observe those rules, do you think that I should regain my health?"

"I firmly believe that such would be the result. Those four rules are very comprehensive. They form a good abstract of the whole science of physiology. God has revealed the laws of health to those who have made the subject their study. We learn that disease is caused by a violation of those laws. If we disobey, we must expect to suffer the penalty."

"Then you do not concur with those who maintain that disease is sent as a judgment for sin?"

Adelaide glanced a moment at her companion, and carefully repressed her inclination to smile.

"Explain your meaning, Delia."

"I have heard people speak of sickness as if it were the consequence of some sin which the suf-

ferer had committed. When our neighbor, Mr.
Wilson, died of the liver complaint, it was more
than intimated by some, that the disorder was a
judgment of Heaven sent because of the man's
dishonesty."

Adelaide laughed, but, immediately after, replied,
with great seriousness, "God has given various
codes of laws. The penalties attached to one class
should not be confounded with those of another.
By his dishonesty, Mr. Wilson sinned against the
requirements of pure morals. The punishment
was, of course, adapted to the offense. He lost
peace of conscience, and the esteem of his fellow-
men. The liver complaint was one of the penalties
annexed to the transgression of a law belonging to
a different code. It has been clearly established,
that exercise is a positive demand of our nature,
which can not be neglected with impunity. Your
neighbor led a sedentary life. Its effects were visible in his painful disease. If bodily ailments were
the result of a violation of the moral law, we should
find that the most virtuous people enjoyed the best
health. Whereas, we know that the openly wicked
are sometimes remarkably free from disease, while
the good are constant sufferers. They should not,
however, be called good, if they adhere only to one
class of laws. By disregarding the rules discovered
for the preservation of health, they disobey the
Author of all law, as much as if they slighted the
commands of the decalogue."

Delia nervously tore in fragments the blue gentians which she had culled from the brink of the rivulet meandering through the wood. She was more deeply agitated than she chose to express. In a low tone, she said, "Those rules do not appear difficult. Could I keep them?"

"Certainly. No commands impossible of observance are imposed by the Creator. But they are not so easy as you seem to imagine. Let us think, for a moment, of the invalid who purchased them at so high a price. Let us fancy him considering those maxims with the intention of strict obedience. The first one enjoined upon him the virtue of early rising. Is that easy?"

Delia shook her head. "Every evening, I resolve that on the next morning I will rise at dawn, but I am seldom up till the sun is high in the heavens. Do you suppose that the invalid was in the habit of lying in bed late?"

"Probably, for morning slumbers are a very prolific source of invalidism. But he was compelled to reform, in order to adhere closely to his new code of laws."

"To rise early now appears to me a very simple achievement, but I know that when the morrow comes, I shall feel as if it were impossible. I resemble the man who spent all the morning arguing whether it were better to rise or to remain in bed. By noon, he determined that the advantages were on the side of rising."

" He should have made his decision the previous evening. On awaking, he should have executed it without pausing for a reconsideration."

" It is very difficult for me to rise."

" You have the full use of your limbs."

" Yes, but the bed is so comfortable."

" But, having enjoyed its comfort for several hours, you might surely desire a different kind of pleasure."

" But rising requires such an effort, especially of a cold morning."

" The effort must, however, be made in the course of the day."

" How is it, Adelaide, that you are always up in good season ?"

" Simply, by rising the moment that I awake, if I see that daylight is beginning to enter my room. Nothing can be easier. The misery of dreading to rise is thus felt only for an instant."

" As you have always been accustomed to early rising, you do not know the pain which it costs."

" Indeed I do. If parents did as they ought, children would not suffer from the necessity of conquering bad habits, or of enduring the evil attendant upon their retention during life. All might be trained to virtue. But as they are not, they should destroy the effects of their imperfect education by themselves forming good habits. In childhood I was accustomed to late rising. I was therefore obliged to overcome the evil by my own exertion. At fifteen it required a great effort. But, do you truly purpose to observe these four rules?"

"Yes; you have given me new motives for action. I know, however, that firm as may be my resolution, this first rule will be very difficult."

"Resolve, then, not to argue the subject in the morning, but, remembering your plans, abide by the decision previously made."

"But, if I linger one moment, I can not summon courage to rise."

"Do not linger. If you should be so unfortunate, rouse yourself without further delay. Repeat Longfellow's 'Psalm of Life,' or Mrs. Osgood's lines on 'Labor,' or Tupper's ode to 'Activity.' You will spring from your couch before reaching the last stanza of any one of these soul-stirring lyrics."

"Alas! to me Tupper's poem on 'Sloth' would be more appropriate!"

"To you, in your present stage of moral progress, but not in that which you intend to attain. Regard it as an axiom, that you can not be well with late rising, and recollect, that unless you wish to die in youth, with this sin unconquered, you must make strenuous exertion for its defeat.

"The next rule for the invalid was, that he should maintain an erect position. You must abandon the rocking-chair, Delia."

"But I am too weak to sit long in a common chair."

"When you are too weak to sit with your head erect, your chest expanded, and your spine so that it shall not curve, you need a change of position. Take a short walk, or a few moments of repose upon your bed. The former will soon be more refreshing than the latter. This second direction to the invalid was rational. A large proportion of disease and debility is the result of actual spinal curvature. Sit and stand upright, that your figure may not become distorted. Throw your shoulders back, that your lungs may not suffer compression. But attention to position alone will not prevent deformity. Exercise, as you will soon see, was also required of the invalid.

"The two remaining rules of that expensive series demanded that the head should be kept cool, and the feet warm. If one of these were observed, the other would demand little care. But, how do you suppose that he obeyed the direction relating to the feet?"

"By wearing warm shoes and stockings."

"You are not like many girls, who persist in slippers and cotton through the winter; but will the warm coverings alone be sufficient?"

"No; for in cold weather I am compelled to sit with my feet before the fire a good part of the day."

"A habit highly destructive to health. The invalid would never have been well if he had thus tried to produce permanent warmth. We should depend very little upon artificial heat. Warmth is indispensable to health, but it should not be exclusively sought from coals and clothing. The fire within should be kept burning. Muscular exercise causes the blood to circulate through the system, so that warmth reaches every part. Those who use their hands and feet a great deal seldom complain of cold. Their blood neither oppresses the internal organs nor rushes to the head in a feverish torrent.

"Another method of securing warmth is the daily use of the cold bath. This is most excellent."

"A cold bath in winter, Adelaide! I should be in danger of freezing."

"Do not incur the risk of such a catastrophe. Avoid bathing in icy water. In severe weather, take the chill from the water, that it may be of the temperature which you would use in summer. The circulation of the blood once regulated, the head may be kept cool and the feet warm, with great ease.

"The invalid was obliged, also, to attend to his diet, and to his literary pleasures. Intemperance in eating or reading causes the head to burn with temporary fever."

"I should not have believed that those four rules were so comprehensive."

"The invalid found that they were not so simple as he had imagined."

"How much exercise ought I to take?"

"Sufficient to promote the due circulation of the blood, and to invigorate you for mental effort. That is a sad state of society, in which laborers are compelled to exert all their power in the use of the muscles, without leaving time or strength for intellectual culture. Take a good walk every day, and spend also a part of your hours for exercise in the vigorous use of your hands and arms. But do you really intend to observe these rules?"

"I do. I will obtain the boon of health, if it is yet within my reach."

"This resolution being made, I believe that you will succeed. Health is greatly influenced by the will. A person of little courage, and of feeble volition, will soon sink under a disease, which would be kept at bay by a spirit of iron determination. I was very much impressed when reading a letter written during the Hungarian strife for liberty. In speaking of Kossuth, the writer says, 'He will not be sick, and he is not.' Resolve that your mind shall triumph, that you will not yield to pain and weakness, and you do very much toward acquiring strength. To this, add a religious compliance with the laws of health, and we shall yet see you well, and even robust. In order that you may fully understand the doctrines upon which I have so lightly touched, you should read some volumes which I have found more fascinating than the most gorgeous romances, namely, the works of Johnson, and of George and Andrew Combe. In various ways will the study of these aid in your recovery. The brain should be exercised as well as the muscles.

I do not wish you to attend to the art of curing serious disease, unless, indeed, you would like to become a physician; but every one should be acquainted with the philosophy of health."

"Have not many lost their health in consequence of hard study?"

"Very little danger would ever ensue if students would remember the motto, 'Be temperate in all things,' and if they would persevere in taking vigorous exercise. Study is essential to the health of the brain. Scholars are injured not so much by their mental activity, as by the anti-physiological habits attendant upon their mode of life. If they would give heed to attitude, pure air, cold bathing, muscular exercise, and seasonable hours, we should not so frequently hear of their loss of health. I fully believe, that in your case a course of moderate study would be highly beneficial."

"Ought I to study any thing besides physiology?"

"Not at present. After a while I hope that you will resume your singing and playing. You must be aware that you have great musical talent. Cultivate it, and you may rival our distinguished performers."

After a few moments, during which Delia's countenance was quite sanguine, it suddenly changed its expression, as she said, "But I am afraid that I have not a good constitution. My efforts will be useless."

"Were your constitution indeed feeble, still

more assiduous should be your care. It must, however, possess some vigor, or it would not have endured so many abuses without giving more serious evidence of injury."

"Adelaide, very healthy people sometimes die after a short illness."

"So much the more do they deserve censure. With an iron constitution and good habits they might have had a long and useful life. What are acute diseases? How are they produced? Fevers and inflammations do not come unsolicited. How common is it to trace even a cold to its source! Carelessness or intemperance of some kind is the cause of such an attack."

"How do you explain hereditary diseases? One can not always guard against those."

"I explain them as my teacher, Combe, has done. The malady was, in the first instance, caused by some violation of law. It then descended from the sinning individual to his posterity. Strict obedience for several generations would insure a healthy race. We are less robust than if all our ancestors had obeyed the laws of health. But, however feeble we are born, if not radically diseased, we can, by our own exertions, obtain a good measure of health. We may, indeed, counteract the tendency to hereditary disease."

"I will begin this evening," said Delia, after a pause of deep reflection. "I will note the date, and see how soon I effect a cure."

"Now, I am confident of your success, but I will give you one caution. Remember your rules, execute your plans, but bestow upon them only so much thought as is requisite for full comprehension. Do not constantly analyze your feelings, and examine your symptoms, or you may become like Miss Leslie's Mr. Gutheridge, who ' attended to no other business than the care of preserving his life by studying to guard himself from all possible maladies and accidents. Therefore, he died of no particular disease, at the age of thirty-four.' "

Delia smiled as she recalled the pleasant story of "The Reading Parties," which had once served to enliven her, when suffering from a tedious sick-headache, and then asked, " Is it not singular that some who are always ill reach advanced age ?"

"Thus it appears at the first view. Hannah More was frequently under the dominion of head-ache, yet she had a very long as well as a useful life. When we see an instance of that kind, we must consider that the disease does not seriously affect any organ. The patient had sufficient vitality long to preserve life, although on very hard terms. When we subtract the numerous days passed in pain and comparative inefficiency, we can not say that such a life is truly long. If Miss More, in her weakness, labored so much and so well, how much more might she have accomplished had she possessed health and vigor! Both may yet be yours."

Delia's eyes were now bright with anticipation.
"I will try to be well," she observed, "that I may
fill some noble sphere."

"That is a good motive. Allowing for rest and
recreation, which all need more or less, we should
exercise body and mind to the full extent of which
they are capable. Do you not remember those
beautiful lines in 'Festus?'

> "'There is a fire-fly in the southern clime
>   Which shineth only when upon the wing;
>   So is it with the mind : when once we rest,
>   We darken.'"

XVIII.

CONCLUSION.

"Oh! backward-looking son of time!
The new is old, the old is new,
The cycle of a change sublime
Still sweeping through."—WHITTIER.

THIS is the last day of January. It is bitter cold. A day on which a walk is an act of sublime virtue, and a cold bath a deed of moral heroism. For water we have ice. The air seems all oxygen. On a day like this I think of the Esquimaux as martyrs, and of the Greenlanders as witnesses to Nature in her most terrific forms. Yesterday the wind wailed in dirges. To-day there is a still, solemn cold, yet more appalling to the thought, reminding one of sailors clinging to the frozen ropes of their ship, and of travelers stifling in the snow-drifts, beyond "the care of the pious monks of St. Bernard." Last night came the Frost-King in his power. On the window-pane is the mark of his icy fingers.

I lay down my pen, draw near the fire, and think of my friends at Clinton, those with whom I passed last summer's happy months.

If ever again I have the felicity of spending a

season in the country, may I find a resort as picturesque as Clinton, and friends as dear as those with
whom I then formed acquaintance.

I have received letters from all save Adelaide.
She has, indeed, sent messages in the epistles of
the others, and promised a missive filling so many
pages that its length shall amply compensate for
its delay. With this anticipation I rest content.

Ella's letter was very entertaining, giving me an
account of all the news of the village, and revealing such extravagant hints of her own future
destiny, that my first impulse was to check the exuberance of her spirits, by reminding her of the
disappointments even of those most distinguished
upon the historic scroll; but, recollecting that hope
was a better leading star than fear, I wisely desisted.
She will learn too soon that the world can not be
moved by her unaided strength. Her empire will,
however, be large. It should satisfy the most
aspiring.

Delia's health is slowly but steadily improving.
It will soon be confirmed. Her will, whatever has
been thought to the contrary, must have had much
original strength; for, having once begun to act
with energy, she has resolutely persevered. For a
few weeks, great indeed were her struggles. Every
morning, the couch, with its tempting repose, its
dreamy influence, was far more alluring than the
beautiful garb with which God at sunrise clothes the
external world. Nor had the wisdom of all the

sages whose records were contained in her father's
library, much attraction for the young girl, as, half
awake, she lingered upon her pillow. But, true to
her promise, she soon learned to rise on first awaking, without pausing a moment to argue the question. She also experienced much trouble from her
confirmed habits of epicurism. But when the rich
pastry and the highly-seasoned meats were offered,
she wisely chose a more simple repast, rather than
the tempting viands and the headache which she
knew must be the result of indulgence.

She has applied herself to the study of music
and to philanthropic schemes. She alternates labor
of one kind and another with rest and recreation,
so that neither body nor mind is overtasked, while
both are in a successful course of training. Inaction is no longer bliss. For the first few days
after her memorable conversation with Adelaide,
her mind hovered confusedly over plans too vast
for her then weak state. She dreamed of Mrs. Fry
and of Miss Dix, talked of Margaret Fuller and of
Madame Roland. Adelaide assured her that she
could not, at present, fill a wide sphere, that she
must be content with a little exertion well employed.
Her main care, for some time, must be her own
improvement. She, therefore, studies as closely as
her health will permit, and confines her efforts for
others, chiefly to Carrie's education, and to the instruction of a Sabbath-school class.

Charles has sent me one letter, consisting of three

pages, two of them filled with a glowing eulogy on Adelaide. Thinking that the document belonged more to that young lady than to myself, I inclosed it in an envelope, and sent it to her that very afternoon.

Even Dr. Leland has deigned to give me quite a long letter. It is a true specimen of conservatism, but I shall value it as a memorial of himself. I shall soon see him, for he informs me of a promise to exchange with Pastor Melancthon in the course of the winter. Ah, he will not be obliged to write sermons that week! I only hope that he will avoid preaching any that I heard from him in Clinton. He can select for that day a couple that were written before I knew of his existence. On entering his study one morning I was amazed to see him fathoming the depths of an antiquated chest of drawers. I saw that they contained vast quantities of dingy manuscripts. With a shudder, I learned that they were his old sermons. He laughed, as he informed me, that, having been invited to preach in Boston the next day, he was desirous of exhibiting the very best of his wares. I demurely offered my assistance in making the selection, but it was decidedly, although courteously, rejected.

Mrs. Leland added a postscript to her husband's letter. The chirography was a delicate cobweb. The doctor probably regarded it as admirably feminine. What a contrast to Adelaide's bold and beautiful style, every stroke of which expresses freedom and energy!

I always looked upon Mrs. Leland as a fit representative of Cornelia, and benevolently hoped that her sons would not think it their duty to emulate the Gracchi.

Captain Wilmot also wrote a few lines on one of his "well days." I was quite a favorite with the old sailor. But, after I had flattered my vanity with this evidence of my power, great was my chagrin to learn that he had fancied me not for my own merit, but, because my father and himself had been messmates during a long India voyage. Of course, my humility returned.

I have received one very comic epistle from Mr. Thornton. I suspect that his book-keeper had the honor of the composition. It was replete with mercantile phrases. I did think of sending to one of old Naumkeag's counting rooms for an interpreter, but I finally decided to understand what I could, and to lose the benefit of what might be merged in the technical terms. The most important intelligence contained in this characteristic epistle was, that my "favor of the ninth inst. came duly to hand." The most satisfactory paragraph intimated that a long visit from myself would afford his family great pleasure. Mrs. Thornton has never sent me one line. I am afraid that the good man forgot what he surely might have remembered with ease, that his wife would not be very much elated with that which she would certainly consider as an incursion. I should prefer to go to Captain Wilmot's.

Although I regarded Mr. Thornton and the young people with great affection, I studiously avoided the lady of the house after one eventful morning which plainly revealed that the state of her attachment for me was far from cordial. In a very frenzy of joy, I had rushed into her parlor, announcing the reception of a letter from Father Cyrus. I had hardly left the room, when Mrs. Thornton vociferated, in a fearfully Stentorian tone, "I wonder whether all the Salemites are maniacs!" Too much amused to be angry, I simply cautioned myself never again to seek sympathy from the ireful matron.

See that carriage rumbling through Walnut Street! Who can be traveling on this drear wintry day? Look at the driver's face! In hue, it resembles mahogany. Its expression betokens stern resolve. The worthy man seems like a veritable impersonation of Boreas. How closely his stalwart frame is enveloped! His head is surmounted by a huge, shaggy cap. His ears are snugly concealed within the folds of a capacious woolen comforter. His chest and shoulders are protected by one of those new-fashioned garments, styled *gentlemen's shawls*. It does not much differ from the ladies' tartans. It has the same Scottish air of warmth and security, denoted by the brilliant plaids worn by the "weaker vessel." If the men assume our graceful apparel, I only hope that they will cease to complain, when a woman fancies the hideous hat, coat, etc., which they claim as their prerogative.

Why, the carriage has even rolled to my own domicile! The driver is pulling the bell as if he were pursued by a score of policemen. I rush to answer the ring, without one thought of the frosty air which I am to inhale on opening the door. Who has come to visit me on such a day! I actually did not know that any one of the human family regarded me with so much affection.

There, the door is open. In furious haste the driver lets down the steps of his vehicle. Out comes Adelaide Wilmot as calmly as if the mercury were ninety degrees above zero. I am so surprised that I can hardly speak the welcome which gushes from my heart. She enters, divests herself of fur, bonnet, and cloak, and sits down by my fireside, ere my eyes have ceased to dilate with wonder. She observes me with a quiet smile.

AUTHOR (*with an involuntary shiver.*) My dear Adelaide, I am delighted to see you, but—

ADELAIDE. You can not imagine why I have come.

AUTHOR. As my very dear friend, you are always welcome. But the day is so remarkably inclement, that I can not regard your visit as a common occurrence.

ADELAIDE. Be not alarmed. This was the day appointed for my journey. You are aware that I never allow myself to be defeated by the weather. My object, however, is not simply a visit. A few days since, papa received notice, that a debt long since due would now be paid on the presentation of the bill. I have come to take the money.

AUTHOR. Had it not been for that debt, I doubt whether you would have left your father even for my sake.

ADELAIDE. You are right. Rose is not quite competent for the charge. But I intend to stay a few days, and inspect the curiosities of Salem.

AUTHOR (*aside.*) I am truly glad to see Adelaide, but I should prefer to entertain her within doors. If I am to play the part of cicerone, I sincerely hope that the weather will moderate.

Spring will soon arrive. You need be in no haste to depart. You did not leave Rose without a companion?

ADELAIDE. Oh, no, Ella is with her, but I must return early next week.

AUTHOR. We shall see. How are my friends, the Clintonians?

ADELAIDE. My father is as well as usual; Delia has nearly regained her health; Dr. Leland has broken a ligament in his left foot. The others are free from illness.

AUTHOR. What occasioned Dr. Leland's accident?

ADELAIDE (*with indignation.*) Some of his spasmodic movements, I presume. If people were careful, they would not suffer from casualty.

AUTHOR (*with a nod of assent.*) Is he able to preach?

ADELAIDE. He might preach, if he could walk,

or even ride. But he is compelled to stay at home, and attend to the position of his foot. His parlor would hardly contain the congregation.

AUTHOR. Who supplies the pulpit?

ADELAIDE (*biting her lips.*) The Andover students come in turn. We have a new one every Sabbath.

AUTHOR (*with deep sympathy.*) Stay with me, Adelaide, till the doctor has recovered. You shall hear all the varieties of city preaching.

ADELAIDE (*with a comic air of denial.*) Not I. My curiosity is excited to see and to hear those prospective clergymen.

AUTHOR (*aside.*) Now, Charles Thornton, beware, or Adelaide may begin to think "Rev. Mrs." a title not to be despised.

But, Adelaide, I dislike students' sermons. The young gentlemen appear as if they were never again to preach. Their discourses are a complete medley, touching upon every topic in the whole scheme of Christianity, and giving a clear view of none. Their manner, too, is beyond endurance. They either scream as if the hearers were deaf, or, so tremble with diffidence, that their voice is almost inaudible. I am unwilling to hear any man preach, till he has bade farewell to the Theological Seminary, and has begun to think and act for himself.

ADELAIDE. Send your remonstrances to the professors who have the care of the candidates. But I am in haste to communicate my plans. I must return in a few days. Before I go, I intend to see all the wonders contained in your "holy and beautiful City of Peace."

AUTHOR. "Holy and beautiful." My friend, that was a mere flourish of Rufus Choate's. Beauty is, however, a characteristic of our city; but, to see it in its perfection, you should come in summer. Salem is unique. It combines the advantages of both town and country. Its "shade-trees and flower-gardens" are renowned. Then, also, a walk of a mile or two, in almost any direction, will disclose scenes as picturesque as those which travelers have wandered far to behold.

ADELAIDE. Yes, I am aware of that fact. I must see them all. You shall take me to Kernwood.

AUTHOR (*a chill pervading her frame.*) Kernwood is indeed a Paradise—in June. I am not in the habit of exploring it at this season.

ADELAIDE. I must have a draught from Cold Spring.

AUTHOR (*shivering.*) Cold, indeed, in January.

ADELAIDE. I must ascend Witch Hill.

AUTHOR (*with a ghastly smile.*) Witch Hill is attractive for its historic associations, but it is a place which, for the honor of my native town, I am averse to exhibit to strangers.

ADELAIDE. Were you to level the hill, you could not obliterate the disgraceful record. I will also visit North Rock.

AUTHOR (*imagining herself standing upon this*

celebrated rock, at the mercy of the winter wind.)
The view from North Rock is very fine, but I
believe that King Æolus reigns upon the sum-
mit.

ADELAIDE. I must wander through Harmony
Grove. Can it compare with Mount Auburn?

AUTHOR. No, indeed. Harmony Grove is distinguished by a quiet beauty. Its scenery has not
that sublimity, that funereal grandeur, which so
deeply impresses one at Mount Auburn; nor are its
monuments so magnificent. Our cemetery can,
however, boast some fair landscapes, and a few fine
memorials. In *summer*, it is a pleasant resort.

ADELAIDE. I must cross North Field Bridge, and
see the route which the disappointed British took in
their retreat.

AUTHOR (*her teeth chattering, while she thinks of
that locality as the coldest spot in Salem.*) Should
you attempt to pass that bridge on a day like this,
I believe that your retreat would be far less reluct-
ant than Colonel Leslie's

ADELAIDE. I have long desired to see Fort
Pickering.

AUTHOR (*shuddering, as she looks through a
slight rent in the picture of the Norwegian Mael-
strom, which the Frost King last night painted on
the window.*) Fort Pickering commands a splendid
seascape. In summer, nothing can be more delightful than to ramble over the rocks, to gaze upon the
distant lighthouse, and to watch the ebb and flow of

the cool waves. But, my dear Adelaide, you forget that the chief beauty of all these scenes must be sought when,

> "The wild flowers bloom, or kissing the soft air,
> The leaves above their sunny palms outspread."

Come a few months hence, and you shall see them in festal array. Let us spend this visit in reading and conversation.

ADELAIDE. A part of the time. But I must see Salem.

AUTHOR. With regard to storms, I am as heroic as yourself. I can bear all kinds of weather save intense cold.

ADELAIDE. If you have such a dread of the cold, you will never equal the celebrated Mary Margaret Kirch, who discovered a comet, and published a treatise on the approaching conjunction of Jupiter and Saturn.

AUTHOR. Mary Margaret's fame will never be mine. If I obtain distinction, it will not be in astronomy, unless, like the first votaries of that science, the students upon the Chaldean plains, I could have a beautiful climate for the pursuit of my investigations. Now, when I am abroad of a winter evening, I merely cast one loving glance toward the Pleiades, and wonder what has become of their lost sister; or, give one look of admiration to Orion, as he gleams forth in his glory; and then hasten home, to attend to those branches which can be pursued by the fireside. My studies, this winter, do not call me to survey the stars for practical illustrations. But, Adelaide, the weather will certainly be warmer next week. Our climate is fickle. Even the morrow may be moderate, so that we can take one excursion. I will not go to-day.

ADELAIDE. To-morrow, then, we will commence; you, as guide; I, as stranger. To-day we will converse. What were you doing on my arrival?

AUTHOR (*disposing of her writing implements.*) I was thinking, or musing. I had been scribbling.

ADELAIDE. Is your book finished?

AUTHOR. Not quite.

ADELAIDE. During my visit, you will read to me what you have written.

AUTHOR (*aside.*) What would Adelaide say if she knew that my last summer's adventures form the material of my book?

ADELAIDE (*raising her voice.*) H——, you will read it to me?

AUTHOR. Excuse me, my dear. You shall not hear one line till all the rest of the world have the same privilege.

ADELAIDE (*gently twirling a terrestrial globe which stands upon my table, and significantly glancing at the revolving countries.*) All!

AUTHOR (*modestly.*) Those of the American people who read my productions.

ADELAIDE (*her longing eyes following the retreating manuscript.*) If I might hear one page.

AUTHOR (*determined to change the subject.*) Not

one. Now, Adelaide, I have a charge against you. Did you not promise to send me a long letter?

ADELAIDE. Three weeks since, I redeemed that promise.

AUTHOR. I have received no letter from you.

ADELAIDE (*With ludicrous manifestations of horror.*) That letter! Why, H ——, it contained twelve pages! I prided myself on the generosity of my disposition, which induced me to write so much for your gratification.

AUTHOR. Twelve pages! What a loss! You deserve the title of "indefatigable paper-crosser." May not a letter so cumbrous have been intercepted, as likely to contain the outlines of some Gunpowder Plot? It must have attracted attention. I will see the post-master. It may yet be found.

ADELAIDE (*with an air of stoicism.*) It has probably wandered to some other Salem. The result of my labor will be burned at Washington, with other ill-fated epistles.

AUTHOR. It can not be lost. I will take measures for its recovery. Lest, however, it should not be found, you may orally give me the contents.

ADELAIDE (*with deliberation.*) Knowing that no subjects would interest you more than those which we discussed last summer, I filled my letter with an account of a long interview that I had had with Dr. Leland.

AUTHOR. Oh, Adelaide, tell me every word!

ADELAIDE. I am undecided. Even after I had

been so good as to commit the whole to paper for
your service, I half regretted that I had thus done.
Concerning your request for a verbal communication, I can think only of Cowper's complaint of
those who,

> "Echo conversations dull and dry,
> Embellished with 'He said,' and 'So said I.'"

AUTHOR (*warmly*.) No conversation between
Dr. Leland and yourself could be "dull and dry."
I am very eager to know its purport.

ADELAIDE. I have no serious objection. Soon
after his accident, I had the civility to call at the
parsonage. He was comfortably established upon
the sofa, having a table filled with books and papers
within reach. The expression of his countenance
was a singular combination of patience and irri-
tability. On seeing me, he joyfully exclaimed,
"You are welcome, Adelaide. I should not soon
have found time for a long conversation with you,
had it not been for the occurrence of this misfortune."

He did not once ask me whether or not I had
leisure for a protracted call. The clergy always
appear to think that they are the only economists of
time. Turning to his little daughter, he said,
"Minnie, run to Captain Wilmot's, and tell him
that Adelaide will spend the afternoon at my house."

He seemed to regard me very much as a deserter
or a fugitive slave whom he had happily secured.
I could not avoid laughing, as I said, "I will remain

with great pleasure. You need not be so precipitate."

Mrs. Cornelia, as you call her, probably surmised that I was doomed to receive a private lecture, for she soon left the room, merely desiring her husband to send for her if his foot gave him any trouble.

"Adelaide, you were a very modest, prudent little girl," was Dr. Leland's singular commencement, "but I am afraid that you are becoming quite the reverse."

Certain that I could be charged with nothing truly unfeminine, I earnestly begged to know the reason of his fear.

"You are very bold, Adelaide, in the expression of your ideas. You give them utterance without due premeditation."

"You misjudge," replied I, warmly; "I am always careful to study both my thoughts and words, and to weigh well their consequences. Can it be proved that, because my conclusions sometimes differ from your own, that they are erroneous? May not your views be wrong?"

Dr. Leland was a little amazed at this presumption, but he merely said, "Very well, Adelaide, I intend to talk plainly this afternoon, and I will not withhold from you the same privilege. I can no longer be silent with regard to your course. Worthy of admiration as it is, in many respects, in others, it loudly calls for censure. With deep anxiety have I observed your tendency to error. As your spiritual guide, I must interpose some check upon your progress. Better that you now hear reproof from me, than that you wait till you must receive it from the whole community."

Despite my usual self-possession, it was not wonderful that I trembled on hearing these ominous words. From a child, I have loved and revered my pastor. This actual rebuke gave me pain, the more that it was wholly undeserved. As soon as I could command my voice, I said, in a low tone, "Sir, I have long wished to converse with you on certain topics. You have not given me the opportunity. Respecting some subjects, however, I knew that your opinions were irrevocably formed, and that it would be useless for me to argue with you."

The clergyman assumed a patriarchal air.

"My dear Adelaide, for you to argue with me would indeed be folly. It is your place to listen to my instructions."

Being thus ranked with Rose, Ella, and all the other children of his charge, I almost laughed as I thought of myself sitting there meekly to receive his dictation. He looked at me with a very grave countenance, on which, however, I had the satisfaction to detect a lurking smile.

"Adelaide," he resumed, "I am afraid that you are deviating very far from the right path. You are quite an ultraist. You are strangely latitudinarian. I do not ask you to repeat either creed or catechism. But you must tell me whether your

views of doctrine are still those of the church which
you were early taught to believe held 'the faith once
delivered to the saints.'"

"In all that even you would consider fundamental," was my prompt answer, "I firmly agree.   I
occasionally think that some points are pressed too
far.   I often wish that I could know more of Schleier-
macher, whose opinions were more nearly allied to
those of the evangelical party than to the rational-
ists', but who could not exactly subscribe to either."

Dr. Leland closed his eyes as he said, "Schleier-
macher was far more evangelical than many would
have us believe.   But you know quite enough of
him.   I shall not dwell upon this subject, for I
believe, my child, that, in doctrine, you are not
alarmingly heretical.   Probably, no two persons
have precisely the same views.   There was a time,
indeed, when I thought you slightly Pelagian.   You
appeared to place too much stress upon act, and too
little upon faith.   That I may be certain, however,
you may express your opinions upon that topic."

Thus summoned to give what, in reality, was
my creed, I hesitated a moment.   A bright thought
soon occurred.   I recited the lines,

"'Therefore love and believe; for works will follow spontaneous,
Even as day does the sun; the right from the good is an offspring,
Love in a bodily shape; and Christian works are no more than
Animate love and faith, as flowers are the animate springtide.'"

The pleasure which he first evinced, on hearing
this reply, was soon clouded.

"Your theology is correct, Adelaide. The poem which you have cited is beautiful in style, sound in doctrine, if we may judge from Longfellow's translation. But why go to a bishop? Could you not give an answer from the words of one of your own denomination?"

"Dr. Leland, to me it is immaterial who is the author of a sentiment characterized by truth and beauty. I would receive it even though from the pen of an infidel. I should view it as a proof that his heart was not wholly beyond reclaim."

Dr. Leland was slightly disturbed. After a short pause, he remarked, "I am afraid that you are not a true Congregationalist. You often speak with great disrespect of the attempts of the laity."

"If I ever thus speak, it is because the performances of some of the number are worthy of contempt. Is not that usage shameful, which commits the conduct of public religious exercises to men, incompetent to teach even a common district school, to initiate the young in the mere rudiments of learning? How can such be expected to lead aright the devotions of others, or to give, in their so-called exhortations, any instruction deserving of the name?"

"Adelaide, Adelaide, are you an Episcopalian?"

"No, sir. In form I am as tolerant as in doctrine I am rigid. I regard ceremony as of very little consequence. I like the forms of the Congregationalists, Presbyterians, etc., for their simplicity; those of the Episcopalians, for their exceeding beauty. In whatever church I had been born, there should I have wished to remain, unless convinced that it were heretical."

"But, my dear child, form is of more moment than you imagine."

"Of what importance can it be, whether, in endeavoring to pray, I kneel or stand? Cecil found motion the best incentive. His oratory was a walk of twenty paces. Can you think that the form of church government is of any consequence? Are we not told, by those who have investigated the subject, that no complete system can be gleaned from the Scriptural records of the early church?"

"Some thus assert; but I am confident that our Congregational mode is the nearest approach to the apostolic form."

"The Episcopalians will assert the same of their system."

My pastor waved his hand, as if we were needlessly digressing, and said, "You ought never to utter a word in condemnation of the exercises of the lay members."

This was uttered with an emphasis, reminding me of the manner in which the Abbot Dunstan probably domineered over King Edred.

"Not if I think that harm will result from their proceedings?" was my quiet answer.

"What harm?"

"People of good taste and of literary attainment will be disgusted by such attempts at teaching."

"God give them a better temper!" ejaculated the clergyman; "but, Adelaide, you are not a Congregationalist, if you refuse to sanction the labors of the laity."

"I have told you, sir, that I care not for form. But I do not wish to be compelled to listen to ignorant men."

"But, think of the absolute dominion which the clergy of the church of England possess! With your independence, you would not like such a state of affairs."

"I can not tell, sir. Some of our lay-members are educated; others, grossly ignorant. To the necessity of listening to the latter, the former are, in a great degree, subject. It is also painful to be governed by the votes of such men. I must confess, that the authority of the 'lord bishops' would not always be so galling as that of the 'lord brethren.' Numbering the advantages and disadvantages on each side, these two prominent churches are nearly balanced. I should, of course, prefer the one with which my early associations were connected. I have sometimes regarded, with longing eyes, yet another system. If I could agree with the doctrines of the Friends, I should like to join their society, because of the equality of influence granted. There, man and woman are on a level. Each sex is represented. A woman speaks as frequently as a man. But, if I could respond to their articles of belief, I would alter the rule with regard to public speaking.

None of the laity should officiate. Thus, granting that the clergy are educated, we should have no ignorant teachers."

"Persons who have had but few advantages, are sometimes able to give instruction. Bunyan was an ignorant man."

"True; but did not Bunyan possess one order of genius? A person, thus endowed, has the power of benefiting others, whether or not he has been thoroughly educated. Learning, however, would have improved even him. Can not every gem take a polish? When we think of the very few thus gifted, ought we not to make a rule that none shall speak save those who have themselves been taught? If any one is conscious of power like Bunyan's, let him draw an audience for himself. He will succeed. But, in a common assembly, let only the regular guide speak. The enlightened lay members, knowing that they could exert their influence in other places, would willingly be silent, on the consideration that they were spared the annoyance of listening to their unlettered brethren. The pastor of a church might be either a man or a woman, thoroughly fitted for the office."

Dr. Leland raised his hands in horror. With flushed face, and sarcastic tone, he asked, "Why not follow the example of Joanna Southcott, establish a new sect, and stand forth as the leader of a band?"

"I prefer to employ my efforts for the reformation of the sects already established."

"My dear child, what authority exists for your views? Can you point to a single confirmatory passage in the whole Bible?"

"The books of both the Old and the New Testament were written when women were kept in a state of ignorance more shameful than that which now exists. The sacred volume contains all needful religous truth; but should we seek in its pages regulations for the office and deportment of people living at so different a period of advancement? Yet, even in those ages, when, despite unfavorable circumstances, power did break forth, it was acknowledged. We find that Deborah was a prophet. Professor Stuart himself declares, that the ancient prophet, not the priest, held the office now occupied by the Christian clergyman. In an edition of the New Testament, printed in 1574, a woman is mentioned as pastor of a church."

Dr. Leland rather angrily exclaimed, "Where is your proof? Show me the text. What has become of that edition?"

"Sir, is it not probable that very many editions of the New Testament have been published unknown to yourself? I presume that the passage, to which I have referred, in the edition of 1574, was slyly expunged by the jealous male pastors, who were unwilling that women should possess equal honors with themselves. Sir, I am very calm. I am no wild fanatic. I entertain no feelings of animosity toward my brethren, but I do demand my share of the freedom which they enjoy. The sexes differ in physical strength. Let man hew the forest, plough the field, rig the ship. Let woman tend the child, fabricate the garment, perform the household labor. Let the mechanical work of life be thus divided. But, in every sphere which claims the extended exercise of intellect, woman has an equal right. The medical profession has now opened to those females whose inclination thus leads. No woman, who wishes to be a physician, will now be obliged to follow the example of Agnodice. Instruction is freely offered. I firmly believe that, ere long, the other professions, the various kinds of business, all offices of trust and emolument, will be thus accessible. Then woman will not be compelled to toil in some humble sphere for a contemptible pittance, nor to live as a dependent upon the bounty of others."

"My dear Adelaide, pray return to the regions of common sense. You almost wholly overlook the grand sphere of your sex. A woman should marry, assist her husband, and take care of her children."

"But, consider a moment, how far the women outnumber the men! For very many, a single life is unavoidable. Shall they be excluded from every dignified profession save that of teaching? This is indeed a noble office, but it does not accord with the taste of all. What would our liberally educated men say, if school-teaching were the only employment for the exercise of their power? What shall

all these single women do? Rather than sew for a
maintenance, I would become a common servant,
and labor hard from morning till night. What
other occupation is offered to thousands of indigent
women, than the frightful monotony of the needle?
Many unmarried ladies are qualified, or would easily become so, if the opportunity were given them,
for the high stations monopolized by men. Do you
reply, that the professions are already crowded?
What does that prove? Have we not a right to
our share? Besides, a good proportion of the present holders are incompetent, despite their education. Their minds were not worthy of high culture.
Think of unskillful physicians, sending their hapless
victims to the grave! Look at lawyers, as incapable
of an argument, as if they had never heard a discussion, nor perused a single treatise on logic! Hear
the heavy-brained clergymen, whose chief virtue is
that of developing the spirit of forbearance in their
martyred hearers!"

"My child, you distress me beyond measure. I
should be sadly grieved to know that any delicate
woman of my acquaintance was exposed to the stare
of an audience, to the observation of the rude multitude."

"Think a moment, sir. The distinguished Hy-
patia, who excelled even the most illustrious male
teachers of one of the celebrated schools of philosophy in the ancient world; who was regarded as an
oracle by the people; who was consulted, on im-

portant occasions, by the governor of Alexandrea, was never the subject of coarse insult, was never guilty of any thing unbecoming a modest woman. I doubt whether the spirit of bigotry and of jealousy, which caused her cruel death, is yet extinct. I would have no ignorant person of either sex teach in public."

"Leaving the army of single women, for whom you appear so deeply concerned, do you think it decorous that a wife, a mother, should have such prominence before the world? How could she fulfill the duties prescribed for her by God?"

"I see not why married women should not have leisure for public life, as well as for the foolish, miscellaneous objects which often make such a draught upon their time. Why should not a woman, an educated woman, deliver a lecture as well as hear one?"

With a look of mingled horror and disgust, the clergyman answered, "Words can not express my emotions, when I think of a woman, so evidently made for private life, exposed to public gaze. Reflect also upon her physical organization. What compass of voice can she boast?"

"Among men, it is not always the powerful voice which commands the most attention. But, sir, voice depends upon cultivation. In a large hall, Fanny Kemble can make the most remote auditor hear every word that she utters. Respecting your views of the mother's peculiar office, did not Mrs. Fry, despite her large family, spend a great deal of time in lecturing? She was comparatively wealthy. She was not compelled to devote her whole time to bodily labor. The poor mother of many children, all dependent on her exertions for comfort, is generally incompetent for extensive usefulness. We do not expect the common housewife to teach, any more than the common farmer or mechanic. When a woman has been able to procure aid in the requisite household labor; or, when, although not rich, her domestic toil has only served as needful exercise, and has not encroached upon her opportunities for mental improvement, what objection can be raised if she also choose to fill a public sphere?"

Could you have seen the singular expression of Dr. Leland's countenance, as, after a moment's pause, he looked up with the air of one about to offer an unanswerable argument, you would have smiled, even had your mind been absorbed in serious thought.

"Adelaide, two persons might reason upon a subject for years, and neither of them succeed in convincing the other. Why waste our time and strength in disputing, when we can have a 'Thus saith the Lord?'"

"I will not grant that you have any such authority for your views."

"My child, how will you explain those passages in the New Testament which require that women should be silent in the public meeting?"

"I explain them in this way. The Bible contains much that was intended for mankind, even from the time of the record till the end of the world. It also contains much that was designed merely for the passing age. You admit that Christians are not bound by the Mosaic law. They look upon those prolix details in the Pentateuch, as a curious record of the course of training to which God subjected His ancient people. The doctrines promulgated in the early days of the Christian church, were designed to be permanent. Truth is eternal. But habits and customs vary. A mere conventional law would be received by one age, and discarded by another. I believe that the rule which the apostle gave, demanding the silence of women in the public meeting, was founded, not on the law of God, but on the prevailing usages of the times. Have not other primitive injunctions been rejected? For instance, 'Greet one another with a holy kiss.' This kind of salutation was then universal. Church members could thus manifest their affection without any infraction of decorum. But an attempt to comply with that direction would now be highly indecorous. What is proper in one age, is improper in another. Women may now speak with propriety. Kisses—promiscuous—may not now be allowed. Society changes its views."

Had you but seen Dr. Leland's visage! Anger he would have evinced, had he not been overpowered by a sense of the ludicrous. The spectacle of the

youthful sisters of his flock, fleeing from the proffer-
ed kisses of the brethren, flitted before his mental
vision. As soon as he could speak, he replied, in
tones scarcely audible, " My dear Adelaide, I feel
constrained to say, with Mrs. Malaprop, 'Much
thought does not become a young woman!' "

What further proof of Dr. Leland's wisdom I
should have heard, I am unable to determine. At
that moment, Minnie re-entered the room, exclaiming, " Captain Wilmot says that Adelaide can not
stay this afternoon. Her aunt Louisa has come
from Dorchester."

Accordingly, I bade adieu to the clergyman, and
hastened home to meet my aunt.

AUTHOR (*aside.*) That dialogue shall form the
conclusion to " DELIA'S DOCTORS."

The University of Illinois Press
is a founding member of the
Association of American University Presses.

University of Illinois Press
1325 South Oak Street
Champaign, IL 61820-6903
www.press.uillinois.edu